A DATE *with* DEATH

In The President's Service Series: Episode 1

ACE COLLINS

Elk Lake Publishing

In the President's Service, *Episode One: A Date with Death*

Copyright © 2013 by Ace Collins

Requests for information should be addressed to:

Elk Lake Publishing, Atlanta, GA 30024

Create Space ISBN-13 NUMBER: 978-1-942513-13-1

Cover and graphics design: Stephanie Chontos and Anna O'Brien

Editing: Kathi Macias and Kathy Ide

Cover Model: Alison Johnson

Photography: Ace Collins

Published in association with Joyce Hart Agent Hartline Literary Agency.

To Alison

CHAPTER I

Sunday, September 21, 1941
A field in France

Just past midnight, Private Nigel Andrews lay flat on his stomach, hiding in some tall weeds just beyond a French pasture.

The twenty-seven-year-old Liverpool native was a college graduate. Blond and green-eyed, he was stocky, just a touch over five-eight and an ounce short of 150 pounds. But in this situation, size didn't matter.

He was tough as shoe leather and hard as iron. In his unit's boxing tourney, he had whipped men six inches taller and more than fifty pounds heavier. So in spite of his schoolboy appearance, those who knew him never crossed him.

His strength and grit notwithstanding, Andrews had once wanted to become a pastor and was even engaged to a preacher's daughter he'd met at Hope College. But for the moment those plans had been supplanted by a driving desire to get off of French soil alive. His mother and father had already lost one son; they likely couldn't survive losing two. They'd even fought his being drafted.

He hated the military and everything about it. So no matter the odds, he vowed he would survive this unholy war. He also vowed to make sure that whatever it took, short of his death, ultimate victory would be realized.

"Where is that blasted plane?"

Andrews turned his attention from the horizon to an obviously frustrated Col. Reggie Fister. Speaking to no one in particular and likely just yapping to defuse his anger, Fister continued to lash out. "It was supposed to be here and ready for takeoff. Blimey! We do our impossible job perfectly, and the Air Force can't even manage to get the easy part right. Whose side are they on anyway?"

For the past week the elite unit's secret mission in Nazi-occupied France had gone much smoother than expected. After a night parachute drop, they'd met with the underground and gotten the lay of the land. Over the next six days, they observed German emplacements, studied and recorded troop strengths, and photographed two air bases being constructed for attacks on London. There had been a few close calls, but not once during their time behind enemy lines had they been spotted. Now, in the witching hour, just as their mission was supposed to be concluding, the British Air Force plane that should be waiting on this dark, grassy field to take them back home was nowhere in sight.

Just like his commanding officer, Andrews knew that in a mission based on complete precision, this should not have happened—especially to an elite British unit. After all, everything up until this moment had been done just the way the English liked it—by the book and exactly on time. Now everything was upside down. The game was no longer being played by a set of formal rules, and it looked as though they were going to have to ad lib.

His gut churning and a growing fear gripping his heart, Andrews lifted his chest and rested on his elbows in order to study the French countryside. Except for two sheep, it was completely void of life.

"Sir?" Andrews screwed up the courage to ask the question that was surely crowding deeper and deeper into everyone's mind.

"What?" Fister barked back.

"Do you suppose the Jerries shot it down?"

"Could be," the colonel replied. "And that would mess up the whole works, wouldn't it?" He paused a second before adding, "Let's give them some more time. But I sure don't like being hung out to dry like yesterday's wash. Churchill will not be on my Christmas card list after this. Neither will Monty."

"And if the plane doesn't get here?" Andrews asked. "What happens then?"

Fister's grim expression lightened up a bit. "It could be worse, son. I've always wanted to date a French lassie. I'll wager you have too."

Even at the moment when it appeared they didn't have a chance in Hades, Fister's sarcastic humor and positive attitude remained true.

The colonel was the kind of person Andrews both respected and despised. He loved war, seemed to live for it, and relished the moments when his life was being challenged. He all but wrapped himself in the Union Jack and almost shouted out the lyrics of "God Save the Queen" whenever it was played. On top of that, he was a man's man, a no-nonsense kind of leader who never put his squad in unnecessary danger. If there was fighting to do, the tall, ruggedly built, dark-headed, blue-eyed Scotsman would be leading the way. In a different time he would have been a knight on a white horse, charging into battle with a smile on his face and a glint in his eye. Minus the steed, those qualities had been evident all week during this mission. Fister had always been a step ahead, constantly getting his men out of harm's way just before a group of Nazis happened onto their position. It was almost as if he were psychic.

But now Fister was in a place where he had no control. He was helpless, and his forced grin couldn't hide that fact. As badly as Andrews needed to get out of this bloody war and go home, it did his heart good to watch his commanding officer squirm.

Pushing his helmet back, the angry colonel ran his hand through his wavy hair and spat. After checking the horizon, he turned his gaze back to Andrews and whispered, "Don't worry, Nigel. I will get you out of this mess. You'll be kissing your sweet Becky before the sun sets tomorrow."

He certainly hoped that was true. All he wanted was for the fighting to end and for his life to go back to the way it was before. Who really cared about France, Austria, or Poland anyway? Why not find a way to satisfy Hitler so he'd leave the British Isles alone?

The colonel looked toward the other ten Brits who'd

volunteered for this dangerous mission. "Stay low to the ground," he instructed. "The plane will be here soon. The Jerries are not going to spoil this holiday for us. The information we have is too important for us to be left stranded here. I wouldn't be surprised if Princess Elizabeth herself is on board to greet us each with a kiss."

The intelligence they'd gathered was indeed important. Andrews knew that well. But it had the potential to do exactly what he didn't want or need—make the war last even longer. What he wanted was for the fighting to end and for life to go back to the way it was before. Who really cared about France, Austria, or Poland? Why not just find a way to satisfy Hitler so he would leave the British Isles alone?

Realizing it was going to be a while, Andrews figured he might as well get comfortable. Taking off his helmet, he rolled over onto his back and gazed at the clear sky. At this moment on a peaceful fall night, it was hard to believe there was a war raging all across Europe. It was also nearly impossible to imagine this serene pasture in France was in the middle of it. Yet Europe was aflame, the Germans were destroying London piece by piece from the air, half of his schoolmates were dead, and he'd already fought on the African sands and tramped through the French countryside on this undercover mission. And he'd come to know death as well as he knew the streets of his hometown.

Watching the Grim Reaper work had hardened his heart and made him question his faith in God. He knew hell was real, for he had lived there the past twenty-four months, but he was not so sure about heaven. Was there really such a place, and was his brother Bobby looking down on him from there right now? Did it matter? Did anything matter beyond getting the information they'd gathered back home?

"There it is," Fister barked. "Look over to the west; she's coming in now."

As Andrews turned his head to the right, the colonel pulled a large flashlight from his backpack and clicked it on and off three times. He waited for thirty seconds and repeated the actions. The plane began to descend from the sky toward their position.

"Okay, laddies," Fister called out, "our bus has arrived. But don't get too excited yet. Stay on your bellies until she lands and turns around. Only when she comes to a complete stop and the door flies open do we move out."

Rolling onto his stomach, Andrews rammed his helmet back into place and observed the plane's approach. The bright moon meant there was no need to light the makeshift runway; the pilot could easily see it. And the field was plenty long enough for the American-built Douglas DC-3 to land, turn, and take off.

As it dropped close to the ground, the pilot cut the engines and glided in. Andrews smiled; the less noise, the better.

"Hold your spots," Fister called out as the airship almost noiselessly set down in the eight-inch-high grass. The plane taxied a few hundred yards. Then the pilot refired the twin engines and turned the craft around.

As the plane once more came to life, Fister flashed his light three times. A few seconds later the signal was returned, and the metal bird's side door flew open. "Time to go home, boys. Your country will be proud of the work you did here."

Andrews and his friends pushed off the damp ground, grabbed their gear, and jogged toward the plane. They had covered half of the 150 yards to their ride when gunfire exploded from the woods to their left.

A second later, four feet to Andrew's right, Basil Homes screamed and fell to the ground. Blood gushed from a huge wound just below the intelligence officer's breastbone. There was no doubt he was a goner. His life was no longer numbered in years but in seconds.

"Get to the plane," Fister screamed from behind. "Don't stop until you're on board, laddies. I'll hold them off."

With gunfire popping like corn, Andrews felt an urge to grab the dying man and hold him as the life oozed from his tall, thin body. Homes had a wife and kids. He was smart, funny, and charming. Of all people to die, it shouldn't be him. But that was the way war was; the ones who shouldn't die always did. Just like his brother. There had never been a finer lad in the whole wide world.

"Andrews," Fister screamed, "get moving!"

After taking a final look at his fallen comrade, Andrews turned his attention to the plane. As he and the other nine picked up their pace, the colonel dropped to the ground, grabbed his machine gun, and aimed at more than fifty Nazi infantryman who had emerged from the woods and were racing toward his position. As he frantically fought against overwhelming odds, Fister screamed, "Get on that bloody plane, and get the information back to London. Then have a pint for me!"

With the sound of gunfire echoing all around him, and the

DC-3's pilot revving the plane's twin engines, Andrews and the other nine members of the team continued running. Behind them Fister kept his gun blazing, offering at least a bit of cover and a few more moments to get to safety.

Andrews was the last of the group to leap through the aircraft's doors. No one bothered closing the oval-shaped entry as the pilot opened the throttle and urged the DC-3 across the field. While the plane struggled to make speed for the takeoff, Andrews crawled over to one of the small windows and glanced back toward the spot Homes had fallen and where the war-loving, brash Fister was fighting. At least two dozen Germans were lying on the ground, and the colonel was still shooting. But as the woods came alive with the continuous flashes of gunfire, the foolhardy Scot, who was trading his life for theirs, surely couldn't last much longer. In fact, by the time the plane left the ground a few seconds later, Fister's gun had gone silent.

A dozen men had come on this suicide mission, but only ten were returning home. For the military, that would make this undercover operation a huge success. But what kind of success was worth men dying?

"What a man!" Robby Penny yelled over the plane's motors. "Fister saved us all."

Andrews nodded. "He's the man, all right—the kind who treats war like the ultimate game. No doubt he'll be awarded the Viking Cross." He shook his head and grimaced. "Or at least his family should get it. He earned it by killing a bunch of Germans who were drafted into their army just to be tossed out like lambs for the slaughter. I hate this war. I can't wait for it to be over."

CHAPTER 2

Wednesday, March 4, 1942
The White House

Helen Meeker glanced down at her watch. At 8:30 p.m., the White House still hummed with activity. It had been that way since December 7. No matter the time, day or night, the building was always alive with ringing phones, muted voices, and the sound of doors opening and closing.

Somewhere in the background, a radio played a Glen Miller song. Meeker could barely hear it over the hundreds of other sounds filtering down through the building, but what she could make out didn't seem to fit. The tune was too upbeat, too happy, when in Washington smiles were in as short a supply as milk or butter. And no amount of money could buy so much as a grin on the black market. Even the upbeat strains of a swing band couldn't change the overriding dark dynamic that defined today's reality.

The blue-eyed, auburn-haired Meeker had just uncovered information that shook her to the core. That was the reason she was here, sitting just outside the oval office, where she'd been waiting for forty minutes. Though she knew J. Edgar Hoover wouldn't buy it, she felt she had information with major security implications. Problem was, she couldn't pinpoint what they were.

Not having the definitive answer to that question might destroy her case and torpedo her unique request. But her gut was rarely wrong. She had to try to convince Franklin Roosevelt of the need for her to join with an old friend on a trek that might save an innocent man's life. Even at a time when millions of innocent men and women were dying all over the planet, wasn't one man's life worth a bit of time? She thought so. But would the president?

As she crossed her legs, the pump on her right foot slipped off her heel. Meeker put it back on, then fiddled with the blue purse in her lap. Waiting was not something she did well. It was certainly not part of her normal nature. Then again, nothing was normal now. Normal had stopped with Pearl Harbor. Now every day had different demands and goals, and that meant an ever-changing schedule. It wasn't just that way for her; it was like that for everyone at the White House and probably for people all over the globe. And no one's life had changed more than the man she was waiting to speak to now.

Every moment of every day there was a decision FDR had to make. There was no time for evenings off or trips to the country or even a long weekend with his family. He couldn't be away from phones. He always had to be ready, day and night, to make gut-wrenching calls that ended with young Americans dying. It was not a life anyone would embrace. Yet it was what Roosevelt had been given, and he had to deal with it.

When the door to the Oval Office finally opened, Meeker's attention was yanked away from thoughts of pain and suffering and the overwhelming nature of the president's job. Secretary of State Cordell Hull stepped out into the hall, followed by Secretary of War Henry Stimson. Hull hurried by without a word, but Stimson stopped in front of her. The dark circles under his bloodshot eyes highlighted the deep concern on his face as he dug his hands into his pants pockets. After almost half a minute of stark and disturbing silence, the elderly man forced a smile. "How are you today, Helen?"

She clutched her bag, uncrossed her legs, and stood, staring directly into the eyes of one of the world's most powerful decision-makers. "I'm fine, sir."

"Good," the thin man replied. Perhaps it was the strain of his duties or maybe just the hour, but he looked every bit of his seventy-four years. After pushing his right hand through his close-cropped gray hair, Stimson sighed. "Oh, to be young again. Just don't know if I've got the stamina for this job anymore."

"I didn't think you ever aged," Meeker replied with a wink. "At least that's what they say around here."

"Aging happens." Stimson shrugged to make his point. "But only to those who are lucky. A lot of the boys on the front lines aren't ever going to know the trials or blessings of old age. In fact, there are a lot of things they'll never know. Should be a way for the young to stay home and folks who've already lived a long life to go off to battle. At least that kind of war wouldn't last as long."

There was no way to respond to his sober observation, at least none that carried any weight or hope. Meeker nodded in sad agreement.

"By the way," Stimson continued, "the president told me to send you straight in." He pushed a long breath between his lips, then turned without saying good-bye and trudged down the hall. Meeker studied him for a moment before gripping the knob on the most important office door in the world.

Though she'd been in the Oval Office a hundred times and every facet of it was deeply imprinted in her mind, there was still something intimidating about crossing this threshold. It was like no other room in the world. This was the heartbeat of the nation and contained perhaps the last hope of the free world.

Taking a deep breath to steady her nerves, she twisted the knob, silently opened the white door, and entered.

The room's sole occupant, dressed in a black suit, white shirt, and blue tie, sat behind his desk, a stack of newspapers piled on a table to the left. Beside them, fanned out like oversized playing cards, were updates from the various battlefronts. To the right, on a small bookcase, sat photographs of the president's family, including his spoiled Scottish terrier. Meeker imagined Fala had more security clearance than any cabinet officer, and she smiled as she thought of the good times she'd spent in the company of the playful canine. After enjoying a few seconds of happy memories with Fala, she turned her attention back to the man who called this oval-shaped room his office.

The president—his long, thin cigarette holder pinched

between his lips—seemed lost in thought as he stared at a painting on the far wall. Meeker peered behind his wire-rimmed glasses and into his eyes. She sensed Roosevelt's mind was not contemplating the art but was actually a few thousand miles away.

After she had taken a seat in one of two leather-backed wooden chairs in front of his desk, he turned to greet her. "Helen," he said in his clipped New York accent, "I trust you are well." Before she could reply, he said with a smile, "That blue suit looks lovely on you. Have I ever told you you're the spitting image of your mother when she was your age? What a woman she was!"

Meeker nodded. "I remember her spunk. Dad always said I got it in spades."

"That you did, my dear." The president leaned forward on his elbows. "I've often called on you to do a job for me. But I can't remember the last time you came into my office without an invitation. I don't have to be Sherlock Holmes to guess this must be important."

Was it really that important? She'd thought so earlier. But now that she was here, she wondered if what she had to share was worth stealing time from the world's most powerful leader. Maybe not. But it was too late to turn around now. She had to go with her gut and hope he could read between the lines, as she had.

"Mr. President—"

He waved his hand to cut her off. "If I've told you once, I've told you a thousand times—call me Franklin. My goodness, young lady, I've known you your whole life. In fact, you called me Uncle Franklin when you were a child."

Meeker nodded. "Yes, sir." She tried to form his first name with her lips but couldn't. It didn't seem right to be that familiar with the leader of the free world. Instead she skipped personalizing her comments as she pushed forward.

"Sir, about a month ago, I requested a car from the motor pool."

The president's laughter filled the room and echoed off the rounded walls. "You mean that bright yellow Packard you're so proud of finally gave up the ghost?"

She shook her head. "No, sir. My sister was visiting and she needed it for a few days. But I had to follow up a lead the OSS had given me."

"They're proud of you over there. Arthur is begging me to let him have you full time." Roosevelt shook his head. "But I can't do that. There are issues here that I only trust you with."

"Actually, sir, I believe one of those issues is the reason I'm here."

"Well, then, let's hear about it."

She took a deep breath. "The car I got from the motor pool was a 1937 Lincoln-Zephyr sedan."

Roosevelt leaned back in his chair and clasped his hands together. "A great car. I really like the V-12 engine. And that model has great lines."

"The vehicle was seized in an espionage case. It belonged to Wilbur Shellmeyer."

"The Lutheran minister we arrested for spying for the Nazis."

"That's him. He's due to be executed on March sixteenth."

"Sad case." Roosevelt sighed. "I understand he has a wife and three children."

"He did," Meeker corrected. "One of the girls supposedly died about six months ago. The mother and the other two children live in Germantown."

The president tilted his head to one side and raised an eyebrow. "Supposedly died?"

"I'll get to that," she assured him. "On my second day of driving Shellmeyer's car, I opened the glove box and found a notebook containing detailed information about the car's every fill-up, oil change, and maintenance. At first I didn't think much about that. But as the hours passed, my curiosity got the best of me, and I started wondering about a man who would be such a stickler for recording everything."

Roosevelt pointed a finger in Meeker's direction. "Curiosity has killed many a cat, my dear."

"I know," she shot back. "But it's why I'm good at what I do."

"Touché. Now, what did your curiosity lead to?"

"I had to know why a preacher and father would turn spy. So I dug into his case file. In a box of his belongings, I found his Bible, which had countless detailed notes in the margins. He even kept a record of his children's heights in the notes section. The man's journal, which he called a logbook, was just as comprehensive. I can tell you everything he ate at every meal for three years. I know how much rain fell on what days. I can even give you the key points of his sermons and who he visited at hospitals."

"Sounds like a perfect spy to me. Good at getting information, a person people trust, and an eye for details."

"That's exactly what bothers me." Meeker lowered her voice a bit, even though they were alone in the room. "The case against him was pat, but the materials the FBI found didn't have any detailed information. And the code in his notes was so easy to break a child could have done it."

"But didn't he confess?"

"Yes. And that bothers me too. There wasn't enough evidence to hold him, much less convict him, but as soon as our people showed up at his door in response to that anonymous tip, he gave them a stack of documents proving he'd worked for Hitler for five years. It was as if he knew they were coming and was waiting for them. He could have burned that stuff, but he didn't."

The president shrugged. "Maybe he panicked, or perhaps guilt got to him."

"I thought about that." Meeker crossed her right leg over her left, then pulled her skirt's hem down over her knee. "But those confessions didn't fit with the detailed notes I found in his Bible and his logbook. So I went to his church and examined their records. Turns out he was performing a wedding on a day when he claimed he was photographing our shipyards in Norfolk. Another time, when he was supposedly stealing files at Fort Bliss, the church records say he was at a funeral. There are a dozen more examples that dispute what he told the FBI."

"Why wasn't this discovered before?"

"Because he confessed. And because there were photographs

and papers in his home that matched up with what he claimed. No one thought it was necessary to look deeper. And with everything that's going on right now, we didn't want to look a gift horse in the mouth. So we just saddled him up and took him for a ride."

The president rubbed his chin. "But he confessed. As I recall, he offered no defense. He didn't even try to make a deal to give us information on the people he was working with. And if I'm not mistaken, he's said nothing since going to prison."

"Which leads to one of three conclusions. Either he's completely loyal to the Nazis. Or he doesn't want to rat out a friend. Or he's afraid of something even more than death." She locked eyes with her boss. "I'm beginning to think it's the latter."

"One of your hunches?"

"Maybe. But I've discovered something else. His oldest daughter, Ellen, drowned while on a family vacation in Mississippi last October. But they didn't bring her body home for a funeral. The day after the drowning, she was buried in a small rural cemetery in Georgia."

"So?" The president shrugged. "A lot of folks bury their loved ones near where they die. Maybe their grief was so great they felt an urgent need to put matters to rest."

Meeker shook her head. "I don't think so. Every member of the Shellmeyer clan, going back three generations, is buried in the same cemetery in Germantown, New York. Ellen should have been buried there too. And if they couldn't take her to New York, why would they go to Georgia for the funeral? It doesn't make sense."

"Well, young lady, you've certainly set forth a lot of interesting conjecture. I trust you have something more than assumptions."

"I think I do." She got up from her chair and walked to the window overlooking the rose garden. After glancing into the darkness for a long moment, she turned back to her boss. "But to prove it I need to get into that girl's grave."

"Are you crazy? Her family would never agree to exhuming the body."

"I'm sure they wouldn't. But if it were a matter of national security, they'd never have to know."

Roosevelt pulled a cigarette from a box on the desk, pushed it into his holder, lit it, and took a draw. "So, what's your theory about the 'supposedly dead' daughter?"

Meeker moved to the corner of the desk nearest her boss and leaned against the antique piece of furniture. "My guess is that Ellen is being held somewhere by the powers behind this deal. They're buying time until they can pull off something really big. If Shellmeyer talks, she dies. And the pastor is perfectly willing to be executed to make sure his daughter isn't killed."

"That's a pretty wild story, Helen."

"But it's the only thing that makes sense. And my gut tells me this is something we need to pursue. However, I don't want to go through regular channels."

The president looked over the top of his glasses. "Why not?"

"I think there might be a German mole in the White House, though I don't have a guess as to who it is. So I want to do this off the record. I need a cover to make it look like I'm working on something else."

"I'm sure you can make one up." He smiled. "And when you do, I'll issue an official order."

Helen pushed off the corner of the desk and returned to the chair. She reached into her purse, pulled out a letter typed on White House stationery, and placed it in front of her boss.

He skimmed the three paragraphs. "So you want me to grant you permission to interview some experienced law-enforcement officials who might be officer material."

"Yes, sir. I also need something else."

"What's that?"

"Henry Reese."

"Why him?"

"I believe the notes in Shellmeyer's Bible and journal are written in code. Reese can break that stuff down better than anyone I know. Besides, he's a good shot, and I'm thinking there's going to be some shooting before this is over."

Roosevelt set his cigarette in an ashtray and looked back at the painting he'd been studying when she walked in. The room grew still. One minute became two, then three. The ticking of the grandfather clock by the entry grew louder.

After a good five minutes, the nation's leader finally spoke, his eyes still fixed on the far wall. "I wonder how many of our boys have died during our little chat. I wonder that a lot. When I eat breakfast I consider how much American blood has been shed in the time it took for the cook to fix my eggs. How many more died as I went through my morning ritual of putting these braces on my legs, getting dressed, and being moved into my wheelchair? That kind of thinking must seem strange to you."

"No, sir."

"You've made a good case for Shellmeyer's innocence. But those boys who die in battle are innocent too. Their only crime is being too old or too young to be drafted. They didn't ask to die, didn't want to die. But I sent them to a place where they did."

Once more the room grew eerily silent. The clock ticked. And Meeker waited.

Finally Roosevelt's eyes left the painting and met hers. "I can give you what you need. But I can't give Shellmeyer a reprieve unless you get me proof that he's innocent. We can't look soft on espionage agents at this point in the war." He glanced at the calendar on his desk. "You've got twelve days before his execution."

"Then I'd better get moving." Meeker was halfway to the door when he called her name. She turned and looked at him.

"There's something I need you to do as well."

"What's that?"

"I want you to spend some time with a man England has designated as a hero of sorts."

"Excuse me?"

"Let's just say I want you to go on a few dates for your country."

"You can't be serious." The thought of feigning romantic interest in a stranger, especially as a job requirement, turned her stomach. But the serious look on the president's face told her she had no say in the matter.

Resigned to the worst, she returned to the chair and sat down to hear the details of her fate.

CHAPTER 3

Meeker tilted her head and frowned. She couldn't believe the president would ask her to date someone for political reasons. This was not what she had signed up for, not at all.

Roosevelt smiled. "I see I have your attention." He settled back into his chair and pushed his fingers together. "What do you know about Colonel Reggie Fister?"

"The English Viking Award recipient?"

"Yes."

She shrugged. "Just what I've read in the newspapers. He held off scores of Germans while the men in his undercover operation got on a plane and escaped occupied France. The reports I've read indicate the information gathered during the mission led to a number of successful English bombing runs."

The president grinned. "You know the story well. Are you aware of a member of that unit named Nigel Andrews?"

She nodded. "I've seen photos of him with the king and Princess Elizabeth. He was chosen to raise money for bond initiatives and give a few speeches to rally the troops. As I understand it he was the member of the unit who was closest to Fister. So he's kind of serving as a substitute for the dead hero."

"That seems to be the general consensus, yes. Turns out Andrews got promoted to corporal and was assigned to be one of Churchill's personal assistants."

"As a bodyguard?"

"Essentially. In a few weeks, Churchill will be coming here for some secret meetings. No one must know about it. He will be hidden away on an estate in upstate New York. Andrews will be with him while he's here. But to give the illusion that Churchill is still in London, the British corporal will arrive in Washington a few days early. He'll appear at a few bond rallies, do a bit of meet-and-greet, participate in various social events. Whenever he's in the public eye, I want you with him."

"With all due respect, sir, I don't have time to be a decoration on some soldier's sleeve. A man's life is on the line, and I have to get to the bottom of it before we execute him. Can't you hire some Hollywood starlet for the job? The press would eat that up."

"Andrews is a valuable symbol for the Brits, and we have to show England we recognize that fact." Roosevelt's tone was firm. "He needs a beautiful, professional, intelligent woman by his side during his visit. Besides, the gossip you'll create by being a part of my staff will take up far more of the press's time and attention than some starlet would." He took a puff on his cigarette. "This is not a request."

Meeker suppressed a moan. "I understand."

"Good. The first event is in six days, so you've got some

time to get a start on your other project. After that, Mr. Reese can cover for you on the days you're with Andrews."

"Okay." She sighed. "Let me know when I'm needed. In the meantime, I'll do everything I can to get to the bottom of something that's far more important than serving as a dizzy debutant."

Roosevelt's eyes sparkled. "You never know where you might find something important. Your days with Young Nigel— as Winston has taken to calling him—might just open up something that will change your life."

"I don't have time for marriage," she grumbled.

"Who said anything about that?" He laughed. "But as I know you don't fear fear, the only thing you really have to fear is your fear of commitment."

She shook her head. "I'm not afraid of that either. I'm just not the type to bake cakes and darn socks, that's all."

Without giving the president a chance to reply, Meeker headed for the exit. Just before closing the door behind her, she said, "I'll keep you informed on both fronts."

"I'm sure you will." Roosevelt turned his attention to one of the reports on his desk. "I'm sure you will."

The clock in Meeker's head ticked even louder than the one in the Oval Office. She was on a mission, and time was at a premium. A man was going to die if she didn't find out some answers—and fast.

CHAPTER 4

Thursday, March 5, 1942
FBI Headquarters

Dressed in a navy-blue suit and white blouse, Helen Meeker marched into the FBI offices in the Justice Department Building. Having once been on loan to the Bureau, it was a place she knew well. After checking in with the receptionist, she made her way back to the familiar confines of Henry Reese's office. A quick glance through his open door proved his absence.

"You looking for Agent Reese?"

Meeker turned and stared into the dark, scorching eyes of a tall woman with broad shoulders and a dead-serious expression. She was likely between fifty and sixty; her short, curly gray hair framed a square face unadorned by makeup. Her eyes were deep brown, almost black, and her jaw was firmly set. She seemed as warm as a pit bull protecting half a dozen new pups.

"I'm Helen Meeker from the White House."

"I know who you are," the woman snapped back. "Reese has spoken of you the way some folks talk about Joan of Arc. That

doesn't mean much to me. Reese is just like every other man."
She raised her eyebrows. "Impressed more with a good set of
pins and a haunting smile than a solid brain. Well, not me. I've
seen your type before. Just another woman trying to charm her
way into a man's world—and you know what I mean by charm."

"If it's what I think you mean, then you need to go wash your
mind with a bar of lye soap."

The pit bull frowned, crossed her arms, and tapped her right
foot. Meeker was not put off by the assertive manner or harsh
expression.

"I have an order here from the president, which has been
approved by Mr. Hoover, to take Agent Reese with me to
investigate something with national-security implications. Now,
where is he?"

"At the First Continental Bank."

"When will he be back?"

"When the bank robbers free the hostages and are arrested,"
she hissed. "So it looks like your little adventure will have to be
put off for a while."

Seeing no reason to continue the conversation, Meeker spun
around and retraced her steps. As she exited back onto the street,
a thought crossed her mind. *We need that woman on the front
lines. She'd scare the Germans to death!*

CHAPTER 5

As Meeker drove up to the bank, she saw that DC police cars had blocked off the streets around it. She parked in a lot just off Vine. After paying the attendant, she pushed through a crowd of curious spectators and up to the barricades.

The scene in front of her looked like it had been staged for a Jimmy Cagney film. There were no signs of life on the street for as far as she could see. Either the cops had evacuated everyone or folks were staying behind closed doors.

As she leaned farther over the wooden barrier, a uniformed cop, who appeared to be in his sixties, rushed over. "No one gets in, lady," he barked. "We got a dangerous situation on our hands here."

She flashed her smile and her credentials. "I'm Helen Meeker. I need to be taken to wherever FBI Agent Henry Reese is holed up."

"I'm Sergeant O'Hara." The man lifted his hand to slightly above his head. "Is Reese about so high, built like a football player, with a face girls swoon over? Or is he the short, stocky guy who looks a bit like a mule?"

"The former."

"Jackson," O'Hara yelled to a younger cop. "You watch things here. I need to take this pretty young woman to see the FBI men."

As the tall, slim Jackson took up his position, O'Hara led Meeker across the street, down an alley, and to the back of a red brick building. Another cop glanced over her identification before opening the service entrance into a flower shop. He then pointed to a rear staircase.

The cop and Meeker made their way up about twenty steps into a large room with four windows looking out on the bank building across the street. In front of those windows sat two men dressed in suits. One was her old friend and former partner.

"Hey, Henry," she called out. "What has Hoover gotten you into now?"

Reese glanced back from the window and smiled. "Nothing that should concern the president. Shouldn't you be putting sugar in Roosevelt's coffee or taking Fala for a walk?"

"I only draw those details on Tuesdays," she shot back.

The two of them walked to a corner of the room, which Helen hoped was far enough away from the windows that Reese's partner couldn't hear their discussion.

"So why are you here?" he asked.

"The president has issued a request for you to help me with a matter that he feels needs a couple of sharp eyes and good minds. You and I have to get to Georgia ASAP."

"Sounds like a trip I'd want to take," he replied. "But I can't go until we get this mess solved."

"Can't you call in a backup?"

"Nope. I'm the only guy the lead hood will talk to. So until we end this thing, I'm stuck by the phone."

Meeker moved to the window and looked out onto the street. It might have been just an hour before noon on a busy shopping day, but there was nothing moving except one stray dog, who'd obviously found something he liked in a trashcan. He had knocked it over, and now only his back half was visible.

"What's the score?" she asked.

"Three armed men walked into the bank about an hour ago. They demanded all the cash on hand. One of the patrons managed to sneak out the back and called the cops. When two policemen showed up, the robbers locked the door and made their demands. So far no one has been injured. But the situation is a bit explosive."

"What do they want?"

"The usual," the agent next to Reese interjected. "Safe passage to the airport, where we're supposed to have a DC-3 fueled and ready for take-off. Basically, they want to get out without being handed a go-directly-to-jail card."

Reese nodded at his partner. "This is Rod Giger."

"Nice to meet you. I'm Helen—"

"Oh, I know all about you." Giger's eyes fixed on her. "I love the story of you tying Big Nose McGrew to the hood of your Packard and taking him for a ride."

Meeker smiled, but she was determined not to get sidetracked. "So why can't you just go in and take those men out?"

"They have six hostages," the long-faced, droopy-jawed agent noted. "The bank president, two male tellers, and a woman with her two small kids."

"Children change the dynamics," Meeker noted.

"Don't you know it." Giger groaned. "No way we can run in with guns blazing or even use tear gas."

Meeker's eyes shot back to the bank building. She studied the two-story brick building. "How are you communicating with them?"

Reese pointed to a phone on the windowsill.

Noting a stack of newspapers sitting against a far wall, Meeker got an idea. "Call them. Give me a chance to talk to the man in charge."

"Why would I do that?" Reese asked.

"They might be more prone to listen to a woman."

Reese shook his head. "Your sex appeal isn't going to convince them to change their plans."

It worked on you." She followed her quip by batting her eyelids and grinning.

Reese shrugged and picked up the receiver. "Fine. I don't mind watching you hit the same wall we have." After a few seconds, he said into the phone, "This is Reese. I have someone who wants to talk to you. It's a woman."

He covered the receiver and whispered, "The guy's name is Ben. He appears to be the leader. By his accent I'm guessing he's from the Midwest."

Meeker grabbed the phone and took a deep breath. "Ben, this is Helen Meeker. How would you like to visit with a reporter from *The New York Times*?"

Reese and Giger's confused expressions made her smile.

"And why would I want to do that?"

The gruff voice caused Helen to tremble, but she kept her voice steady. "The more the public knows your story, the better chance you have of winning sympathy and getting what you want from the FBI. And if you're in *The Times*, you'll be famous. Warner Brothers will probably want to make a movie about your life. Maybe they could get Gable to play you."

After an interminable wait, he grumbled, "I guess that'd be all right."

"Great. I'll walk out of the florist shop in about a minute. I'm wearing a blue suit. You be ready to let me into the bank when I get there." She hung up.

"What are you doing?" Reese demanded.

"I have a really important job to do, and I need your help. We've got a plane to catch tonight. If I wait for a man to solve this dilemma, it might take days."

"These guys are ready to kill anyone who gets in their way."

"Then I'll try to stay out of their way." Meeker smiled as she turned and hurried down the stairs.

"Helen," Reese called out as he followed, "I don't want you doing this."

"Don't worry. It'll be a piece of cake," she assured him as she hurried toward the front door of the flower shop.

She grabbed the knob, pulled the door open, and walked out in the street before Reese could talk her out of her insane plan.

CHAPTER 6

The sixty steps across Third Street were the longest of Helen Meeker's life. She felt eyes on her from every direction, and she knew a few of those folks had guns trained on her.

On the far side of the street, she crossed between a 1941 Buick sedan and a 1938 Studebaker coupe, stepped up on the curb, and made her way to the front entrance of the Continental Bank. She rapped on the glass. A few seconds later she heard the latch release, and the door eased open just enough for her to slip in. Taking a deep breath, she crossed the threshold.

"You the reporter?" asked a tall, heavy man in a dark suit.

Instead of answering she allowed her gaze to take in the scene. There were no surprises; it looked like every big bank in the country. The large lobby held one long, high counter, a desk with a swivel chair, two filing cabinets, and four chairs for customers. Six teller windows on a wall dissected the middle of the room, and off to the right was the bank president's office. Behind the tellers' cages, on the floor in the corner, the obviously frightened hostages sat huddled together. A hallway on the far side of the room likely led to the vault.

Crouching beside one of the front windows and peering through a tiny opening in the closed blinds was a man who appeared to be no older than twenty. He was dressed in an ill-fitting gray sports coat and blue slacks. He looked scared.

Behind the teller cages, guarding the hostages, was a short, stubby, gray-haired man in a black suit. He held a .38 pistol in his left hand and a cigarette in his right. He seemed as cool as a late fall breeze.

Beside her, gun aimed at her gut, stood a middle-aged man with red hair, a pockmarked face, steel-gray eyes, and a firm, square jaw. He wore a navy-blue pinstriped suit that appeared to be made of silk. He looked more like a bank officer than a bandit.

"I asked if you were the reporter."

"No," she said. "I'm Helen Meeker."

"But you said you were from *The Times*," he growled.

"No," she corrected him. "I asked if you would like to speak to a reporter from *The Times*. I didn't say I was that reporter."

"You lied," he screamed as he shoved the pistol forward.

"No. You assumed." She slowly strolled across the lobby, her heels clicking on the marble floor.

"Are you with the FBI?" he demanded.

"Surely you know Hoover doesn't allow women as agents. I'm from the office of the president of the United States, and I have the credentials to prove it."

All three gunmen stared at her, jaws dropped.

"Now, who do I talk to about working out a deal here?"

"Me," said the one with the .38. "I'm Ben."

"Where's the vault?"

"Down that hall."

"Is it open?"

"Of course. How do you think we got the cash?" He nodded at five canvas bags on the floor next to the front door.

She headed to the far side of the room, her pace steady and fast.

"Where are you going?" Ben demanded.

She stopped and turned back toward him. "*We* are going to the vault. I've got to make sure you didn't get a certain something out of there. Once I can guarantee it's still there, we can talk turkey and get you that plane you want." She glanced at the hostages, who peered at her with guarded hope. "But first, you need to let the woman and her little girls go."

"No one gets out of this bank until we're free."

Meeker folded her arms across her chest. "I am one of the president's most valued employees, and having me here means a whole lot more than having a mother and a couple of kids."

His forehead furrowed, as if he saw the merit in her assessment.

"Call Reese," she demanded. "Tell him you're letting three hostages go. After they're released, I will explain why you stumbled into something that's worth the president helping you get away with the money and your freedom."

Ben studied her face a few moments before looking back to his pal behind the teller cages. "Stan, take the woman and the kids to the front door."

As the older man signaled for the trio to get up, Ben moved to the phone and dialed. "We're letting the woman and her kids go. They'll be coming out in a few seconds. Don't try anything or we'll shoot them in the back and then take out the rest of the hostages, including the woman you just sent over."

The mother, wearing a green print dress and black flats, grabbed the hands of the two blonde girls, both about four years old, and hurried them to the front door. When Stan opened the entry, she yanked the youngsters out into the sunlight. A split second later the door was closed and latched again.

"Tell me when they're across the street," Ben barked to the young man by the window.

A minute later he announced, "They're there."

The leader looked back to Meeker. "Okay, now, what's so important in the safe?"

"You and Stan follow me back there, and I'll show you."

Ben looked across the room to the older man and then back to her. "Why both of us?"

"Because it'll take both of you to open the box."

"What box?"

Helen released a drawn-out sigh. "Look, this situation has FDR spooked. He's more worried about you right now than he is about Hitler."

"He is?" Stan asked. "Why?"

Helen looked around, then lowered her voice. "If the material in that box fell into German or Japanese hands, it would likely cost us the war."

"I don't want to cost us the war," Ben said, a worried look

crossing his face. "I might be a bank robber, but I'm still an American through and through."

"Didn't figure you were anything but," Meeker countered. "But because you picked this bank, those papers are your ticket to getting pretty much whatever you want. Now, where do you want to go?"

"Mexico," Ben answered.

"Mexico it is. I just need to make a call."

"To who?"

"The president."

Ben's eyes widened. "How do I know you're not tricking me, like you did before?"

Meeker shrugged. "I'll let you talk to him yourself if you want."

He nodded at the phone. Helen picked up the receiver and dialed a number few people knew. A few seconds later a familiar voice answered.

"White House."

"This is Helen Meeker. Is the president in?"

As the three astounded hoods looked on, the receptionist connected the call.

"Franklin," she said, knowing he'd be tipped off that things weren't normal by her use of his first name. "I've made it to the First Continental Bank. If we give the three robbers safe passage to Mexico, they'll agree to release the hostages and not give the Exodus Plans to the Japanese or Germans. But to assure them that we'll agree to these conditions, they need to talk to you."

"I knew about the bank robbery," the president whispered.

"Are you on the inside with the men?"

"Yes, sir."

"I ought to strangle you."

"Maybe. But we have more important things to deal with now."

"And you want me to assure them there's something of great value there?"

"I do."

"All right. Let me talk to the man in charge."

Meeker held the phone out to Ben.

He took the receiver. "Is that really Roosevelt?"

"You'll know in a second."

His eyes wide, Ben spoke into the phone. "Mr. President."

Meeker remained close enough to hear both sides of the conversation.

"Ben, I'm disappointed in you."

"Sorry, sir," he answered, a tremble in his voice. "But if you can get me out of this, I promise I'll mend my ways."

"I believe you, Ben. However, if you sell this information to the enemy, we will track you down and make you wish you had never been born. Do you understand?"

"Yes, sir."

"Take the cash. But don't hurt anyone."

"You have my word," Ben replied.

"Let me talk to Helen."

Ben pushed the receiver back to Meeker.

"Helen, are you sure you know what you're doing?"

"Yes, sir," she replied. She hoped it was true.

CHAPTER 7

With the two bank robbers watching her every move, Helen Meeker crossed the threshold of the vault, flanked by a twelve-inch-thick vault doorway. At the back of the twenty-foot-deep chamber lay bags of coins on the left and a wall of safety deposit boxes on the right. When she got to the one marked 1776, she traced the locked drawer with the fingertips of her right hand and nodded.

"I need to make sure the plans are still here. Are either of you good at picking locks?"

Ben nodded. "Stan's one of the best, and he has his tools in his vest. But I promise we haven't taken them."

"I have to have proof," she insisted. "My job is on the line here." Meeker moved back to the entry and stood beside the pair. "The plans are in drawer 1776. I guess you can figure why we chose that box."

"The Revolutionary War," Stan said.

"Yep," she replied. "And if you can get it open, you win the prize—a long vacation in Mexico."

Slipping his gun into his pocket, the older man moved to the back of the vault and studied the drawer. A few seconds later he looked back at Ben. "It'll take two of us. When I get one lock tripped, you'll have to hold the tool until I get the other to release."

Ben glanced at Meeker. "I can still shoot you just as easily from back there."

"No doubt."

Rubbing his hand over his mouth, the big man ambled back to where his partner was working on the drawer.

"Okay, I tripped the first one," Stan said. "Hold this tool just the way it is, and don't let it move."

Ben kneeled down, set his gun on the floor, and grabbed the short piece of wire. As he did, Meeker picked up a canvas bag filled with coins.

"What are you doing?" Ben growled, grabbing his gun and pointing it in her direction.

"Dang," Stan grumbled. "The tool moved. Now I've got to do it all over again."

"What are you doing?" Ben repeated, his gun still pointed at Helen.

She lifted the big bag of coins up to her waist. "I just wanted to see how much they weighed. They're really heavy."

"Well, back up against that far wall," Ben ordered. "And quit playing around."

The bag of pennies still in her hand, she took five long backward steps until her back was against the wall near the door.

"Okay," Stan said, "I've got it tripped again. This time hold that wire until I get the other one unlocked."

Once more setting his gun on the floor, Ben turned his attention back to the drawer. As soon as he grabbed the wire, Meeker wrapped the fingers of her free hand around the edge of the vault door. It moved noiselessly a few inches forward. She stepped quietly through the doorway, then slammed the door shut.

After dropping the coin bag to the floor, Meeker spun the lock, which looked like an old sailing ship's wheel, and smiled.

She retrieved the bag of pennies, slipped off her pumps, and silently made her way down the hall. A peek around the corner revealed that the one remaining bank robber was still in his position, gun drawn and studying the street through the slit in the blinds. Hugging the wall, she slowly advanced toward his position.

When she was inches away from his shoulder, he must have sensed her presence, because he jerked around. But before he could aim his gun, Meeker brought the full weight of the canvas bag full of coins down on his head.

He gasped, then fell face forward onto the hard floor. After kicking the gun from his hand, she dropped the bag, picked up the .38 revolver, and hurried to the desk to call Reese.

It occurred to her that she didn't know the number of the phone he was using. She was about to head out the front door when she spotted a bank deposit slip with numbers scrawled on it. When she dialed those numbers, a familiar voice answered.

"Reese, it's me. I have everything under control here."

"Really?"

"One of the hoods is sleeping like a baby. Let's just say I gave him a bit more change than he was expecting." She smiled. "The other two are locked in the vault."

"How did you—?"

"Never mind that. You just get over here and do whatever you have to do. I need to call the president and tell him my plan worked."

Setting the receiver back into the cradle, she shook her head. Perhaps now old J. Edgar would realize that women really did belong in the FBI.

Looking over her shoulder at the confused hostages cowering behind the teller cages, she announced, "Party's over. You can relax now."

CHAPTER 8

After buckling his seat belt, Henry Reese looked out the airplane's window at the capitol building. Once more overriding the powers at the FBI, Helen Meeker had somehow accomplished the impossible and pulled strings to again make them a team for a mission. But that was the way she was. Just about the time he thought he had her figured out, she pulled another surprise to prove he had underestimated her again.

In her case, he loved to be proven wrong.

As the plane lurched forward, he smiled. He might actually enjoy this midnight flight to Georgia, especially since he and Helen were the only two in the plane beside the pilot and copilot.

As the Army Air Corps C-48 lifted off the ground, Reese turned his eyes away from the landscape outside the aircraft and to the woman sitting across the aisle. He never got tired of looking at her. She was uniquely beautiful. Her long, cascading hair perfectly framed her expressive, deep eyes and high cheekbones. Her full lips, arched brows, and angular nose gave her the appearance of a fashion model, but they also pointed to an intelligence few could fully fathom.

A couple of years before, Reese had looked beyond her beauty and discovered she was shrewd, intuitive, and deep. It was a lethal combination for anyone who might try to cross her. But if she was on your side, it could prove the difference between living and dying. And when he was with Helen, he really felt alive.

As she crossed her legs, displaying athletic calves mounted on thin ankles, Reese's mind flew back to the only time he'd ever kissed her. He could still remember every detail of her soft lips pressing against his. Just thinking about that moment caused his heart to race and brought a flush to his cheeks.

"Are you hot?" Helen asked.

Jerking his eyes to her face, Reese shook his head. He felt like a kid who'd been caught with his hands in the cookie jar.

"Well, you look warm." She had to raise her voice to be heard over the Pratt and Whitney's motors. "Even your ears are red."

He shifted in his seat as he sought for a way to change the conversation's direction. "I'm always flushed on flights. Something about the altitude."

She laughed. "Yeah, we must be all of five hundred feet off the ground by now."

Loosening his tie, he stammered, "How did you get us this flight? I figured low-level employees like us would have to take a train."

She winked. "This was a snap compared to what I did this afternoon at the bank."

Reese relaxed, regaining a sense of control. "You had no

business taking that kind of risk."

She shrugged. "If they hadn't bought my story, they would have had one more hostage. But they couldn't afford to shoot me. If they did, you all would have come in with guns blazing."

"You should have waited," he groused. "Hoover had his best minds working up a plan back at headquarters."

Helen laughed. "I couldn't hold off that long. I needed to get you on this plane."

"So this is all about your impatience."

Helen's face lit up with that perfect Hollywood smile of hers. "More about needing to get a mother and her two kids out of that situation. Besides, I knew I could come up with a plan once I got a feel for the situation."

His eyebrows lifted. "You didn't have one before you went in?"

"How could I? I hadn't seen the landscape yet. You can't clean up a room until you visit it." She kept her eyes fixed on him for a moment. "I saw a picture of you at a banquet with Hedy Lamarr. Some say she's the most beautiful woman in the world."

"I was assigned to that duty," he snapped. "Besides, she's married. She and her husband have invented something that might help us in the war effort. Hoover asked me to take her out while he and her husband talked."

"That's a good cover."

"It's true," Reese retorted. "I bet you'll get stuck with that kind of duty sometime."

She frowned. "Let's not talk about that."

He grinned. "You already have! Who is it?"

She shrugged, clearly trying to act nonchalant. "I have to be seen with some British soldier at a few social events."

Reese laughed. "I bet you're dreading it."

"I am," she insisted, her mouth forming a distinct frown.

He'd hit a sore spot. He enjoyed having something to rib her about. Since he rarely had the upper hand, he pushed harder. "Tell me about him. Is he as good a kisser as I am?"

"How would I know?"

"Surely you remember that night in Illinois when we wrapped up The Yellow Packard case."

She tiled her head. "I vaguely remember something about that. Didn't you give me a peck on the cheek?"

"That was no peck. Gable didn't kiss Vivian Leigh with that much passion in *Gone with the Wind*."

"Boy, are you sensitive. What I meant was that I've never even met Nigel Andrews, much less kissed him."

"Oh." He frowned, realizing she once again had the upper hand.

She reached into her briefcase and pulled out a file. "We can chat about old times later. Right now I need you to look over this material and see if you notice the same holes in the case that I found. And if that doesn't convince you, I have a Bible you need to read."

"What could a Bible have to do with this case?

"I think there's a code hidden in some of the notes in the margins. The Bible was owned by a Lutheran minister named Wilbur Shellmeyer."

"I worked that case."

"I know. But you might have missed something."

More than a bit miffed at the insult, Reese grabbed the file and looked through the report. Within fifteen minutes he realized that Helen Meeker had once again seen something everyone else, including he himself, had missed.

CHAPTER 9

Friday, March 6, 1942
Shady Grove, Georgia

Helen Meeker had never been to Shady Grove, Georgia, a sleepy town located in thick woods along a river named for a former president from Tennessee. From what she'd read about this area, most of the residents didn't have phones, some didn't even have electricity, and a few had yet to install indoor plumbing. Agricultural and lumber work offered enough jobs to put food on the table but rarely enough income to do much else. Poverty was the accepted norm, and the best way to escape it was to join the military. Thus, with a war going on, there were very few young men left in the town or the countryside around it.

After the flight landed at Atlanta in the wee hours of the morning, she and Henry had grabbed a couple of hours sleep at a tiny motel. Following a quick breakfast, they had taken one of the FBI's two-door Fords on the hundred-mile trip to Shady Grove. By the time they parked the five-year-old sedan in front of the local sheriff's office, Meeker had fully shared with Reese her theories on the case. If he was convinced about what was—or wasn't—in Ellen Shellmeyer's grave, he didn't show it. In fact, he stayed strangely quiet until the moment they arrived in the small town.

"You okay?" she asked as he switched off the motor.

"Fine." He paused for a moment. "Actually, I'm not. I'm stuck here in the States while all my friends are overseas. They're doing the grunt work, taking the risks, and I'm essentially laying low and playing it safe. Hoover won't let me go into the military, and it chaps my hide."

"We need people here too." Meeker rested her hand on his arm. "In truth, you might be doing work that will keep your friends from dying."

"Not so far," he grumbled. "School crossing guards save more lives than I do."

"I have a suggestion."

He looked at her with a hint of hope in his eyes. "What's that?"

"You want to really help the war effort?"

"You know I do."

"Then get Hoover to send your secretary to face off against the Germans. Sixteen-millimeter artillery shells would likely bounce off that woman's hide."

Reese chuckled. "I take it you met Agnes."

"I left before she challenged me to a wrestling match, so I

didn't catch her name." She grinned. "Now, we have a job to do here, so let's get started."

Armed with two .38s and a presidential order, they climbed out of the sedan and made their way up wooden steps to the slightly elevated concrete sidewalk. As Meeker smoothed her dark blue skirt and adjusted her matching wide-brimmed hat, she looked around at the dozen or so stone buildings that made up the business district.

"Not much going on around here," Reese said. "I feel like we've stepped back in time to 1922. I haven't seen a dozen Model Ts all parked on the same street in years. Our car is the newest one here."

Meeker watched three small children tag behind their mother into a feed store. "This is one of those towns the Depression still calls home. Sad. But, since my social calendar is about to get filled up with a man who salutes the Union Jack, let's get this over before I have to head back to Washington."

Reese chuckled. "I can't wait to see pictures of you and the Brit in *Life* magazine."

"I'll be sure to autograph a copy for you," she grumbled. "Come on, let's get to work."

Meeker led the way into the small structure that housed the area's only law-enforcement officer. The single room was as stark as the main street and almost as dusty. Yellowed wanted posters hung on one wall, a file cabinet sat against another, and two cane-bottomed chairs parked in front of an ancient mahogany desk. Sitting behind stacks of magazines, empty tobacco tins, and a half-eaten sandwich was the man in charge, reading the

Grit newspaper.

In his fifties, the sheriff was perhaps six-two and weighing in at likely 280 pounds. He had graying dark hair and wore wire-framed glasses. His double chins were clean shaven, and he wore a gray shirt and slacks.

Evidently deciding his guests were not going to leave, he finally set the newspaper to one side, lifted his green eyes to study the two strangers for a few seconds, and then, with considerable effort, pulled his large frame off the wooden swivel chair.

"Brice Johnson's my name," he said, his tenor voice drenched in a southern drawl. "Who might you folks be?"

"I'm Henry Reese, with the FBI." After flashing his credentials, Reese cocked his head toward his partner. "And this is Helen Meeker, special assistant to the president."

"The president of what?" Johnson almost spat as he spoke.

"The United States. Name's Roosevelt. You might have heard of him."

"Oh, I heard of him," the sheriff growled. "But I didn't vote for him. He's too uppity for me. I could never trust a man who smokes with a cigarette holder."

"I don't think that'll bother him much," Meeker observed with a wry grin.

The big man shook his head. His expression made him appear more bovine than human. "What brings you down my way? Nobody of any importance has been to this place since President Davis raced through here trying to evade the Yanks. By the way, given the chance, I would have voted for him."

Meeker pushed up onto the toes of her high heels. "We need

a couple of men to do some digging for us."

Johnson shook his head, his cheeks wobbling like jelly. "What do you mean by digging?"

"Dirt," Meeker explained. "We need to dig up a grave at the Grove Cemetery."

The sheriff's eyebrows rose. "You paying?"

"We are," Reese assured him. "And we have a court order for the exhumation."

Johnson nodded. "There are a couple of colored boys, the Wilson brothers, who could do that for you." He narrowed his eyes. "Mind if I ask whose grave you're digging up? After all, this is my town. I have a right to know."

"You can ask," Meeker said, "but we aren't required to tell you. And I doubt the FBI or the president believe you have a right to know any more than you already do. Now, where can we find the Wilson boys? And who do we talk to about getting into the cemetery?"

The sheriff stood up straight. "I don't take that kind of talk from a woman."

Before Meeker could jump down the ill-mannered man's throat, Reese intervened. "I wouldn't recommend crossing her. This woman brought in Big Nose McGrew single-handedly. You might have read about that in the *Grit*."

As the color drained from his face, the sheriff's eyes darted to her. He rubbed his throat as if trying to push out a frog. "You the one that strapped him over your hood like a deer?"

Meeker rocked back on her heels. "That was easy compared to the bank robbers I nabbed in Washington yesterday." She crossed her arms. "Now, who's in charge of the cemetery?"

Words came tumbling out of Johnson's mouth like rocks sliding down a Georgia hillside. "Mort Graves is the undertaker. And before you ask, that's his real name. He's in charge of the graveyard too."

Reese grinned. "Sounds like he was born for that job. We'll need him to be there when we do ours."

"Mind if I go too?" Johnson asked.

"You can be there," Meeker said, "but you can't talk about what we're doing to anyone. You got that?"

"I can keep a secret," the sheriff assured them.

"If you don't, there'll need to be a special election in this town, because your mail will be forwarded to a government facility in Leavenworth. Do you understand?"

The big man nodded.

Reese buttoned his gray suit coat, smoothed his black tie, and pulled his white shirtsleeves over his wrists, all without taking his eyes off the squirming but conciliatory lawman. "Got a place to eat in this town?"

"They fix sandwiches down at Jenkins Cafe. Got a jukebox you can play there too. Only a nickel per song. I love Dinah Shore."

"Sounds good," Reese replied. "While Miss Meeker and I have some breakfast, you round up Graves and the Wilson brothers, then meet us at the restaurant. We'll buy all of you something to eat."

Johnson shook his head. "Mort and I can eat with you, but they don't serve colored folks in the café. So the Wilson boys will have to wait outside."

"They will join us today," Meeker said, her tone firm, "or none of us will be eating."

"But—"

"No buts. I don't care how things are done here on most days. Today the team that works this case will eat together. You got that?"

"Yes, ma'am," the sheriff replied.

Reese turned toward the door. "You make whatever calls you need to make, but be sure to alert the café that there'll be new rules in play today." He grinned. "And if they want to argue about that, tell them they can take it up with the gal who got Big Nose McGrew. You got it?"

The sheriff nodded.

"And Johnson?" Reese pointed to the six wanted posters tacked on the far wall. "Three of those men are dead, and the others are in prison, so you can pull them all down."

The big man scratched his head. "When did that happen?"

"We got the first two in 1937. The rest of the cases were closed a bit more recently—1938."

"Wow. I just put them up last year."

Meeker moved toward the door, but turned before exiting. "We'll see you at the café as soon as you round up what we need. And remember, don't tell anyone what this is all about."

Stepping out onto the sidewalk, she glanced at her partner. "He clearly doesn't have much respect for anyone who's not local."

Reese laughed. "I get that a lot. Comes with being in the

FBI. State cops almost always look at us as either invaders or interlopers. And you know how they feel about women. But your taking down McGrew set the table for this gig to be played by our rules. I wish J. Edgar could have seen that."

CHAPTER 10

Helen Meeker enjoyed the fried ham, scrambled eggs, and toast at Jenkins Café. But never had such a simple breakfast created so much interest. Folks from all over town came in to watch the Wilson brothers eat at a table with white folks. It likely surprised more than a few when the building didn't collapse during the meal.

After eating their fill, Meeker, Reese, Mort Graves, Sheriff Johnson, and the Wilsons climbed into four vehicles and made the mile-and-a-half trip out to Grove Cemetery.

The century-old rural graveyard was typical of those found in almost every state in the Union. The stones were modest, and only a handful of the graves were adorned with flowers. There were a few scattered trees. On the north side of the grounds stood a small frame chapel, its white paint peeling and its tin roof showing a hint of rust. The six-inch-high grass growing in the path leading to the front door of the twenty-by-thirty-foot building revealed that it was rarely used.

Under cloudy skies, Meeker looked the undertaker in the eye. "Mr. Graves, I believe that last October you sold a grave to some folks from up north, a Lutheran minister and his wife. Their name was Shellmeyer."

Graves, a slightly built man in a dark suit and white shirt, nodded. "I did. Quiet folks. Kind of nervous, as I recall."

Meeker gazed at a stone well to the right of the chapel, wondering how best to explain their objective.

"So," the sheriff said, his high-pitched tone displaying his impatience, "is the preacher's grave the one we're going to dig up?"

She shook her head. "He's still alive … at least for a few more days." She pointed toward the chapel. "What's that building used for?"

"We hold services there during bad weather," Graves explained in a deep, rhythmic baritone.

She looked into the man's sunken, dark eyes. "What's inside?"

He shrugged. "About what you'd expect. A few pews, a piano, a podium."

"Does it have power?"

"We aren't as backwoods as you might think. Got a bathroom too."

The dark sky had been threatening rain all day. If the clouds let loose before they finished their work, at least they'd have a dry place to examine the body.

"Where is the plot you sold the Shellmeyers?"

Graves extended a short, bony finger. "About forty feet beyond that maple tree, toward the back of the property."

"Did you do the embalming work on their daughter?"

"No. Never saw the body. They came here with it already in the coffin."

That fit with the scenario she had imagined. "Was the Shellmeyer family alone when they arrived?"

"Let me think." Graves stroked his jaw. "Besides the two other daughters and the parents, there were two middle-aged men. They did most of the talking. They weren't from the South, I'll tell you that. Sounded a bit like my cousins who live up by Chicago."

"Was there a graveside service?"

"Not much of one. The father just said a prayer, and then the two of us lowered the coffin into the grave. They all stayed while Amos and Zeb here tossed the dirt on it. Then one of the middle-aged men gave me money for the headstone they ordered. That was it."

Meeker studied the Wilson brothers. They were solidly built, wide-shouldered men in their forties. Clean shaven, they dressed in flannel shirts, bib overalls, and brown work boots, and had crossly cropped hair. Amos was a touch over six feet, his brother a bit under. Knowing the reason they had been called to this place, they both held shovels.

Meeker addressed the brothers. "Were either of you within earshot of the Shellmeyers at the graveside?"

Amos cleared his throat. "We was both near enough to hear the prayer."

63

"Kind of a strange one it was," Zeb added.

"In what way?"

The young men looked at each other. "It was short," Zeb said. "And it sounded less like a prayer for the family than a warning. I never heard anything like it at a funeral, and I've been to a lot of 'em."

Reese took a step closer. "What made it sound like a warning?"

Zeb's eyes widened. "I'll never forget. The preacher said, 'Please, Lord, let her body rest in Zion's graces, and let no man ever disturb this vessel, for if they do, they will meet you sooner than later.'"

Meeker hurried past the maple tree to the plot the undertaker had pointed out. The white stone marker was simple and direct. It listed only the name, Ellen Shellmeyer. There was no date of birth or death.

Meeker grimaced. The pastor's wish for eternal rest was about to be rescinded. It was time to see if her theory was right.

CHAPTER II

It took almost an hour for the Wilson brothers to dig deep enough into the Georgia soil to strike pay dirt. By that time a light rain had started falling, and the brothers' boots were caked with red clay.

As Helen Meeker looked on from about ten feet behind the marker, the Wilsons succeeded in getting ropes around the coffin's rails. Then, with Sheriff Johnson's help, Graves and Reese managed to wrestle it out of the ground and to a resting point beside the open grave. As the men paused to catch their breath, Meeker approached the coffin, circling it twice to make sure she had viewed it from every possible angle. It was a standard-sized, fairly ornate, gray casket with a rounded top and silver rails. As she had picked out her father's coffin not many years ago, she was familiar enough with them to realize this model was anything but cheap. It hardly seemed the choice a minister with two other children would have made. Because it had been in the ground for such a short time, the sides, where the rain had started to wash away the clinging clay, still showed a shine.

"Mr. Graves," Meeker asked, "what can you tell me about this casket?"

The small man wiped his brow. "For starters, it's much nicer than anything I carry. Nobody around here would lay out the kind of money it takes to buy one of these. You could purchase a new Ford or Chevy cheaper than this."

"Do you know who made it?"

"The Batesville Casket Company of Indiana. You can see their name on the end. They've been around a long time. They're one of the top names in the industry."

She nodded. "How difficult is it to open?"

"Just takes a special key. I've got one with me. Since this one hasn't been in the ground too long, it shouldn't take any time at all."

Meeker stooped and studied the two places the key would fit, then glanced at the sky. The clouds were getting darker, and the rain was picking up.

"Let's get this thing inside the chapel," she suggested. "I don't want the body in this casket getting wet before we examine it. I'll help the Wilsons on this side. You three get on the other side."

After all six had taken their positions, Graves directed, "Lift on three. One, two, three!" Motivated by rain that was now falling hard, they managed the trip to the chapel in a minute or less.

The makeshift pallbearers braced the heavy box against the

step railing while the undertaker checked the ring of keys he pulled out of his pocket. When he finally found the key to the building's only door, they brought the coffin inside the musty building.

"Let's take it up by the podium," Meeker suggested.

After they arrived at that spot, they turned the box so it was parallel to the pews and placed it on the wooden floor. While Reese walked back toward the entrance to snap on the lights and close the door, everyone but her took a seat on the front pew. Only the Wilsons were not breathing heavily.

"You want me to unlock it now?" Graves asked.

"In a moment." Meeker ran her hand along the lip of the box, pausing at a point just above one of the two locks.

"Why is it so important to look at this body?" Johnson asked.

"We need to make sure it's her," she explained.

"Why wouldn't it be?"

Meeker lifted her gaze and directed her answer to all the men. "If Ellen Shellmeyer died in a swimming accident on the Gulf Coast, why bury her here? This wasn't her hometown, and the Shellmeyers had no obvious connection with Shady Grove."

"So what?" Johnson grumbled. "What difference does it make where some kid's buried?"

Meeker tilted her head. "If your father had been accused of being a Nazi spy, it might make a lot of difference."

The sheriff's eyes widened. "Do you think they might have buried important papers with the girl? Could we be sitting on something right here in Shady Grove that might help bring down the Nazis and Japs? Or maybe it was gold or cash."

"I don't know about anything being inside," Meeker replied, frowning as she noted the red clay caked on her navy pumps. "But I do think there's something important that might be revealed here that could help us in the war." She moved her eyes from her soiled shoes to Mort Graves. "How many people are buried in this cemetery?"

"Maybe three hundred. Counting the really old graves, might be double that."

"How many of those are from places other than Shady Grove or the area around here?"

The undertaker shook his head. "None that I can think of." He paused. "No, I take that back. There was a salesman who died back in 1933. We couldn't find any family, so we buried him here. If I remember correctly, he had a heart attack or stroke. He's resting up the way about a hundred feet."

She looked back at the coffin. "Interesting."

"Well, let's get this box open and take a look inside." Johnson rubbed his hands together and grinned. "This is better than Christmas."

Meeker ignored the enthusiastic sheriff's impatience and turned to her partner. "Henry, have you got that photo of Ellen?"

He reached into the inside pocket of his coat and pulled out a four-by-four snapshot. He handed it to Meeker. She studied it for a moment, then looked toward Graves. "Unlock it."

"Now we're cooking," Johnson almost shouted. "Get moving, Mort."

The undertaker fished into his pocket, pulled out a large key ring, and moved toward the casket. He bent over and examined the lock toward the foot of the box, chose a key, dropped to his knees, inserted it, and gave it a twist to the right. The lid released and raised a fraction of an inch. He moved to the head of the coffin and repeated the process with the same results.

"You want me to lift the lids?" Graves asked.

"Before you do," Meeker said, "what kind of shape do you think the body will be in?"

"If it was embalmed, and the mortician did a good job, it'll be easy to tell if it's the girl in that photo."

"And if it wasn't embalmed?"

"Still should be able to do it, though there'll be some decomposition." He looked at the box. "The lack of air in the sealed coffin slows the process down. And this casket wouldn't allow much humidity in, if any. But seeing as how there's no smell oozing out after breaking the seal, I'd have to believe she was embalmed."

"All right, then. We might as well see what we've got."

Graves reached for the front of the lid, but Meeker grabbed his wrist. "Wait a second."

Johnson stood from his spot on the pew. "We've wasted the better part of the afternoon doing this. Let's get moving and see what kind of secrets we find in there."

With rain peppering the tin roof, Meeker studied the oversized sheriff and the eager undertaker before turning her attention back to the coffin.

Graves rose to his feet. "A dead body can't hurt you, lady. There's nothing to be scared of."

"I'm not scared," Meeker replied as she crouched by the

casket. "I just don't like the feeling I'm getting."

"Hogwash." Johnson groaned. "Women don't have the stomach for real law-enforcement work. Never have and never will."

Johnson's opinion grated Meeker, but that was the least of her problems at the moment. Her hunches were usually good ones, and something told her she didn't need to rush into finding out what was inside this box.

She walked to the back of the coffin, then moved back about five feet away to get a full view. The sheriff uttered a curse and all but leaped up to the casket. Before Meeker could protest, he grabbed the lip of the lid and jerked it up.

As he and Graves stared inside, Meeker's ears picked up on a sound she knew all too well. "Get out of here!" she screamed.

Her gut told her she didn't have time to make it to the door, so she hit the floor, rolled over onto her back, slid under a pew, and scooted across the dust-covered wood toward the front wall. Above her the Wilson brothers took three long strides and jumped through a large glass window. Reese, who was closest to the door, had the quickest route out. By the time Meeker had pulled herself under the third pew and was reaching for the fourth, the agent was opening the door.

Meeker peeked out through the aisle and saw Graves, still at the coffin, staring into the open box. The sheriff stood beside him, frozen in the same position.

Before she could shout another warning, an explosion rocked the chapel. Meeker ducked for cover under the pew.

The deafening roar, though lasting only a few seconds, shook the rafters. It blew out five windows and splintered the first two pews, knocking the next one onto its side. The podium was blown into a thousand pieces, and the metal coffin was turned into hundreds of shrapnel-fueled rockets, flying at light speed across the width and breath of the structure. Large sections of the tin roof fell to the floor, allowing the pouring rain inside the building.

For almost ten seconds the sound rocked Shady Grove, and then there was silence. That silence spoke even louder than the blast.

CHAPTER 12

Her ears ringing, Helen Meeker stared at the gash on her right arm. A sheet of tin rested on the pew above her, blocking her view of the sky and shielding her from the pouring rain.

Rather than shove the shredded metal panel away, she grabbed the pew and pulled herself to the back of what was left of the small structure. Pushing to her knees, she took a deep breath, then got to her feet.

Just as she managed to stand, Henry Reese stepped through the open door. Except for being soaked, he seemed fine. Apparently he'd gotten out soon enough to escape injury.

He knocked a sheet of tin out of the way and moved to her side. "You okay?"

"Yeah. Except for a nasty ringing in my ears." She glanced toward the front of the chapel, where parts of the coffin rested between two men, lying on the ground. She didn't have to check the sheriff's pulse to know the consequences of his slow reactions. His body had been sliced to pieces and tossed against the right wall.

On the other side of the room, Graves was covered with blood but he was still breathing. Pushing through the wreckage, Meeker worked her way to the man's side. Bending down, she grabbed his hand.

"Mr. Graves," she whispered as she leaned near his horribly lacerated face.

"There was no body," he moaned.

"It was a booby trap." She glanced over her shoulder. "Henry, get some help. This man needs a doctor."

As Reese rushed out the door, Meeker returned her attention to the undertaker. She pressed her hand against a large wound just below his neck in an effort to slow some of the flow and give the man a few more moments of life.

"Don't bother," he whispered, his thin, almost blue lips forcing a smile. "I know when a person is beyond help. Besides, death doesn't scare me. I'm more than ready to sing with Jesus. I just hope he'll forgive the fact I can't carry a tune."

"My partner went to get some help," Meeker assured him. "You hang on."

"Nothing to hang on to," he said. "But I do want to know something."

"What's that?"

"Why would anyone turn a casket into a bomb?"

Meeker shook her head. "I don't know, at least not yet. But I think it has something to do with why a man waiting for an execution is willing to die for something he didn't do."

"But what happened to the girl?" The undertaker's breath came in gasps.

Meeker was formulating a way to answer that question when the man's eyes rolled back and his mouth gaped open. Graves was dead.

As Meeker stood, Reese reentered the chapel. "The Wilsons are on their way to get help."

She shook her head. Unable to help the dead man, Meeker studied what was left of the casket.

"Did you see what caused the explosion?"

"No. But I know it was a grenade. When Johnson yanked the lid open, it pulled the pin."

"How did you know if you didn't see it?"

"I heard the ticking." After glancing at the two dead men, she added, "Shellmeyer's cryptic prayer wasn't answered in the way he'd hoped, but his fears were realized. Can't say we weren't warned."

"Was there anything else in the coffin?" Reese asked.

"Graves said there wasn't a body. He lived long enough to tell me that."

"Is that what you expected?"

"I didn't think Ellen was dead, but I wasn't anticipating a bomb." She turned her eyes toward her partner, her emotions a jumble of fear and confusion. "This is even bigger than I thought. Shellmeyer knows something with major consequences, and the key has to be finding his daughter and getting her to safety."

"Miss Meeker?" a voice called out from the chapel door.

She looked up and saw Zeb Wilson, appearing none the worse for his experience. "The doctor's coming."

"No reason now. The other two are dead. But thanks for your

help." She paused. "Is your brother all right?"

"We're both fine. Got out in the nick of time. The good Lord was watching over us. He surely was."

Meeker moved carefully through the debris to the door. "Zeb, can you tell me once more what the preacher said when he prayed over the grave?"

He nodded. "I'll never forget it." Zeb looked back toward the gravesite. "He said, 'Please, Lord, let her body rest in Zion's graces, and let no man ever disturb this vessel, for if they do, they will meet you sooner than later.' He was sure right about that last part."

"There was nothing else?"

"No, ma'am, that was it. Expect that he added an 'amen.' And then the folks left, and we covered the casket. Sure wish it had stayed covered."

"Thanks, Zeb." She patted his arm. "You might as well go now. Nothing anyone can do here."

"Guess we'll be digging two more graves," he murmured. Then he turned and walked down the steps.

Meeker turned to Reese. "Shellmeyer's notes in that Bible or the logbook have to mean something. Let's get back to Washington and start digging."

As the two walked down the steps and through the rain to the car, Meeker thought about her last visit to the president's office. He had warned her that curiosity killed the cat. She still wasn't sure about the cat, but there was no doubt it had led to the death of a small-town Georgia sheriff and undertaker.

CHAPTER 13

Saturday, March 7, 1942
Washington, DC

Just past six in the morning, the plane carrying Helen Meeker and her partner touched down in the capitol. She'd had two hours sleep since Thursday, had barely escaped being blown to bits, and had taken six stitches in her arm, but the answers she got on her trip to Georgia only created more questions. Worse yet, the clock was running, and Shellmeyer would meet his maker in just over a week. That gave her very little time to operate.

Yet even with her mind whirling, she had to sleep. Two minutes after arriving at her apartment, she dropped into bed without even removing her clothes. She immediately fell into a heavy slumber that offered both escape and peace.

At four, her ringing phone yanked her from a dream that included a romantic date with Henry Reese at a posh New York nightclub. He'd just asked her to dance when she emerged from the fog, crawled across her bed, and reached for the receiver. Even as she answered she could swear she still heard the strains of the nightclub's orchestra.

"This better be good," she mumbled into the phone.

"I hope you found what you needed in the sunny South."

After rubbing her eyes, she looked at the clock and sighed. Couldn't the president have waited until tomorrow or even tonight?

"Well, sir," she began, hiding as best she could her displeasure with his timing, "I found out enough to feel certain I'm right about Shellmeyer. But I don't have the proof you need. Still, I'm going to get it. Reese has the logbook and the Bible right now. I'm hoping I'll have something concrete for you by Monday."

"Glad to hear that. Now, you need to get yourself fixed up really nice. You have a formal evening at the British Embassy tonight."

"What? I thought my arranged dating life didn't kick off until toward the middle of next week."

"Change in plans. The Brits have scheduled a banquet tonight for about a hundred guests, and you'll be representing the White House. It's formal, and you'll be sitting with Nigel Andrews. I'm sure there will be lots of press climbing all over one another to get a picture of you two. I see this as an opportunity for an arms-across-the-ocean kind of thing. People love that."

"When did this come up?"

"Winston called me from London an hour ago. He said there was going to be some kind of huge surprise announcement during the banquet. When that happens, you need to be on the arm of our hero. And if the British corporal wants you to kiss him on the cheek, do it."

"That's just great," she groaned.

"Be there at seven. And look your best. Thanks." He didn't give her time to respond before hanging up.

After pulling herself out of bed, Meeker wandered over to the dresser mirror and gazed at her reflection. Her face looked more like the Wicked Witch of the West than one that belonged to a member of the social elite. Her hair was still filled with dust from the chapel explosion, her makeup was smeared, and she had huge circles under puffy eyes. Turning toward her bathroom, she wondered if three hours would be enough time to transform herself into Cinderella. She doubted it. Still, her country called, and even if this was something trivial, it went with the job.

CHAPTER 14

Having heard the evening was supposed to be cool, Helen Meeker chose a long-sleeved, jade-green dress with a high neck and low back. She added long white gloves to hide her stitches, a gold necklace, green pumps, and a fur wrap. After driving her Packard through the massive gate and onto the embassy grounds, she parked, presented her identification, and made her way up to the front entry of the stately red brick building at 3100 Massachusetts Avenue.

The embassy seemed to be a cross between a city library and an English country mansion. The columns gave the building somewhat of a Roman look. The rest of the structure clearly showed its British roots.

Walking through the front door, down the hallway, and into the banquet hall, she caught the eye of a dozen men of all ages. As she paused at the entry, four formally dressed males nearly tripped over one another racing to her side. A heavyset fellow, about fifty, with silver hair and a red cummerbund, won simply because he avoided a parade of waiters carrying drinks to a group of twenty or so guests visiting by a massive fireplace.

Meeker waited for the other three to make it to a position in front of her before smiling at the winner and posing a question none of the men likely wanted to hear. "Could you direct me to Corporal Nigel Andrews?"

The member of the quartet closest to her shook his head and frowned. "Oh, that's the way you are. *Pip, pip*, so be it. Can't win them all, your know." He looked toward the other three and announced, "I'll take this." After they left, he introduced himself. "I'm John Babcock, of the Brighton Babcocks." An elderly gentleman, he sported a distinguished handlebar mustache and wore a long-tailed jacket.

"I'm Helen Meeker, of the official White House dating pool."

After bowing he took Meeker's hand and led her to the far side of the room. There, by a side table, stood a handsome young man who looked quite dashing in his dress uniform.

"Nigel," Meeker's temporary escort announced, "this woman wishes to meet you." Babcock leaned closer to him. "Your fortune and my loss." After a final forlorn look at her, he headed back to the entry.

"You must be Miss Meeker," the soldier said in a Liverpool accent. "I've heard a great deal about you, but no one mentioned how beautiful you are."

She smiled. "Did they make you practice that line for very long?"

The Brit grinned. "Let's just say they wrote it for me and

taught me how to deliver it properly. But it wasn't a lie; you are a devastatingly lovely woman."

"Thank you. And I can honestly say that it's nice to spend the evening with a man who can legitimately be called a hero."

"Oh, I'm not so sure about that," he said, his smile fading. "I was just one of the blokes who was lucky enough to get back."

"That's every soldier's goal," she assured him. She was about to ask about the decorations adorning his jacket when she felt a tap on her shoulder.

"Might we have some pictures?"

As Meeker turned, she came face-to-face with a half dozen members of the press corps, ready to record this moment in history. And record it they did. It was a good thing film wasn't being rationed. For the next five minutes flashbulbs popped, and a series of meaningless questions were asked and answered.

When the first wave of the press finally moved off, Meeker suggested, "Let's step out on the patio for a few moments. That might give us a bit of peace and a chance to get to know each other."

After crossing the room as quickly as decorum allowed, the pair escaped through a set of French doors into the cool evening air. Shutting the doors behind them blocked out much of the noise coming from inside the hall.

"This is far better than being in a stuffy room," he noted, "listening to that string quartet."

"Much," she agreed. "So, do you know what this quickly tossed-together affair is all about?"

"I don't. I was touring the DC sights this morning when I

got the word. But it must be something big. The embassy staff has pulled out all the fine china. Still, I wish I was somewhere else." Apparently sensing he'd said something wrong, he added, "I don't mean I don't appreciate being with a beautiful woman like you."

Meeker held up her hand and grinned. "You're fine. I understand. This tore me away from something too. But, since you're not putting the moves on me, like most men in uniform seem to be doing, I'm guessing you have a girl back home."

He got a faraway look in his eye. "I do. Becky's cute, kind of short, and doesn't know much about sophisticated gatherings like this one. But she's all I need or want."

"Good for you." Meeker patted his arm. "She sounds pretty special."

"As special as the first robin in spring. Would you like to hear more about her?"

"I'd love to. As long as she's not a part of the Brighton Babcock clan."

"What?"

"Nothing." She swallowed a smile, feeling a bit sorry for her weak attempt at humor.

As only a British man could do, Andrews took Meeker's elbow and guided her to a railing overlooking the grounds. After glancing up at the sliver of a moon, he began his tale of romance. "I met Becky in grammar school. I still remember that day. Her hair was fixed in strawberry curls, and she wore a fluffy blue dress. The first thing she said to me was, 'You're a might strange sort.'"

Meeker laughed. "I take it she wasn't impressed."

"No. She wouldn't give me the time of day until we were in our teens. But on a fall night in October, at a school party, we danced for the first time, and my heart has been dancing ever since." He chuckled. "That's sounds silly, doesn't it?"

She shook her head. "It sounds nice. No, better than nice. It sounds wonderful."

"You know what's so special about Becky?"

Meeker waited for him to tell her.

"It's the way she ..." He shook his head, his brows drawing together slightly. "I'm sorry. It actually hurts to talk about her."

"Why?"

"Because of this stupid war. It killed my brother. It killed my best friends. It demolished the home I lived in as a child. It destroyed some of the greatest buildings ever constructed in Europe. And it hasn't helped my relationship with Becky."

Meeker wondered how the war had affected their relationship—other than keeping them apart, of course. But it seemed too personal a question to ask.

"We should just give Hitler Europe and make peace. I don't think France would care about Great Britain if the Nazis were leaving them alone. And I doubt anyone would have gotten too upset if Russia had invaded Germany. Who would have come to their defense? But rather than seek peace, we fight. We slaughter innocents and bomb civilians, and there are men who love every moment of it."

Meeker frowned. "You can't be serious."

"The men calling the shots treat people like equipment. Life means nothing to blokes like Reggie Fister."

"Fister?" She gasped. "He was your friend, your leader. And your country's biggest hero."

"He was a lover of war." Andrews's voice took on a bitter tone. "He lived for battle and women. He bragged about his conquests in both areas. Oh, he was charming all right, and he had a wealth of courage and spunk. You would have liked him—every woman did. But he was the kind of guy who draped himself in the flag and looked for ways to prove his manliness."

"Is that bad?" Meeker asked. "I mean, aren't those the kind of men we need right now?"

He looked her in the eye. "If there were no men like Reggie, there wouldn't be any wars. No, we need people who realize that being with loved ones is far more important than killing men who have their own loved ones waiting for them at home. Someone should tell Churchill that."

"You're working for him," Meeker reminded him. "Perhaps you can tell him."

"He won't listen. No one wants peace."

"I do. And so do many others. However, saving Europe from Hitler is of monumental importance. We cannot allow him to make a mockery of freedom."

"I understand why you think what you do. Maybe if you had been there, as I have … if you had known the French arrogance and the—"

The double doors opened. "Nigel," a staff member called out.

"Yes?"

"They're about to make the announcement. You two need to come back inside."

Meeker tucked her arm into the crook of Nigel's elbow and allowed the bitter Brit to escort her back into the banquet room.

"We're supposed to sit at that table," he whispered, leading her to a place near the podium. He pulled out her chair. She had just taken her seat when the British ambassador to the United States stepped up to the microphone.

"Ladies and gentlemen, distinguished guests, and members of our military, on behalf of the king and the British Government, as well as the entire Allied forces, I am here tonight to share a tale of one of the bravest men ever to wear the British colors. You all know his story. One of those here tonight, Corporal Nigel Andrews, served with him in Africa as well as on that secret mission in France. You have no doubt all read of the way Colonel Reggie Fister held off hundreds of German troops so that his men could escape back to England and share the intelligence they uncovered on their mission."

Meeker glanced at Andrews and noted his face was twisted in an expression of both pain and anger. This tribute to a fallen hero, a man he evidently neither cared for nor admired, was likely too much for the resentful man to stomach.

"Tonight," the ambassador continued, "I have additional news to share with you about Colonel Fister. But why should I deliver this report when there is a man far better suited for that duty?"

The ambassador paused, waved his hand toward the side of the room, and smiled. "Ladies and gentlemen, may I present to you Colonel Reggie Fister."

All eyes went to a door as it opened, and a distinguished-looking man in uniform stepped into the room. As those in attendance jumped to their feet, clapped, and shouted out greetings, Meeker's eyes fell back to her escort. Andrews had not risen, and he was not clapping. Rather, he looked stunned beyond belief.

CHAPTER 15

An hour after the meal, and more than two hours after he'd been introduced, Colonel Reggie Fister finally escaped the onslaught of press and fawning dignitaries and made it to the table where Helen Meeker sat with Nigel Andrews.

Andrews had said almost nothing the whole time. The unbelievable news that his dead friend was still alive seemed to have put him in a near-catatonic state.

"Nigel," the black-haired, green-eyed hero called out as he approached. "My, it is good to see you."

Andrews looked like a frightened rabbit as he awkwardly rose from his chair and saluted.

"None of that," Fister barked. "Open up those arms and give me a hug." Showing none of the normally stiff English reserve, Fister grabbed Andrews in a bear hug and almost squeezed the life out of him. He then stepped back and announced with a wide grin, "You're looking good, lad."

"Thank you, sir," Andrews mumbled. But the wild, nervous look in his eyes remained.

If Fister noticed his friend's apprehension, he didn't show it. Instead he turned to Meeker, allowing his eyes to slide from the top of her head to her pumps and back up. "My goodness, this one is beyond what I dreamed of when the underground was nursing me back to health."

She smiled, not sure whether she should feel complimented or repulsed, and extended her hand. "I'm Helen Meeker."

"Helen, eh? I believe the name is Greek for *torch* or *flame*. And beauty like yours would likely set any man's heart aglow. If I survived everything I went through in France only for this moment, it would be more than enough." He caressed her gloved hand.

Fister was a combination of English charm and American brashness with a hint of Scottish rogue. He was like no one Meeker had ever met. If he didn't come off as such a gentleman, his leering gaze would have made her uncomfortable. But he had been away for a while, and likely he would want to be in the company of any single woman. So for the moment she could forgive him. And forgiveness was easy when a man was as attractive as Reggie Fister.

"Miss Meeker," Fister sighed more than said, "is there is a place we can go and get to know each other better?"

She shook her head. "I'm not familiar with the embassy. This is only my second trip here." She glanced at the ashen-faced Andrews. "Nigel, do you know of a spot?"

The corporal swallowed hard and nodded toward a door just across the entry hall from the banquet room. "There's a small study that's likely not being used right now."

"Perfect," Fister announced as he continued to stare into Meeker's eyes. "Nigel, why don't you lead the way?" As the corporal stepped out, Fister took Meeker's arm and tucked it into his. "This makes being turned over to the Americans by the underground all the better."

"You mean you haven't been back to England yet?" Meeker asked as he led her around tables toward the study.

"No. When I was rescued, they felt it best to debrief me here in the States. I will get to head home when the delegation that Nigel is a part of goes back." He smiled, his eyes shining like lighthouse beacons. "And suddenly I have no problem with that delay. In fact, I hope it goes on for months."

Meeker could almost feel her cheeks flush.

Andrews opened the door and pushed on the lights in the study. As he did so, Meeker's eyes were pulled from Fister's dynamic smile to the room. It was no more than twenty by twenty, with bookcases lining all except the far wall—which, based on its French doors, likely bordered a garden area. There was no desk, but the room contained a half dozen high-backed green leather chairs. Judging from the lingering smell of cigar smoke, it was likely a place where the staff gathered for relaxed, after-hours conversations.

The colonel led her to a chair on the far side of the room and took a seat directly across from her. Without a word, he watched her movements as she crossed her left leg over her right knee and folded her hands in her lap.

After almost a minute of awkward silence, Andrews moved to a chair on her right and finally spoke. "Colonel, I don't understand how you escaped. When I looked out the plane's window, the woods were filled with Germans, and you were out in the open."

"Ah." Fister grinned. "And thus begins a story that is part miracle and part the nature of German arrogance." The Scotsman leaned forward in his chair and folded his hands over his right knee. "When I quit firing, they assumed I was dead. One man came up and rolled me over, and I played the part. After checking on poor Homes, their commander ordered one of his men to find a local farmer to take care of the dead limeys. I stayed there, not moving, with Germans all around me, for at least a half hour. Finally some sleepy-headed old man showed up and the Nazis moved off. When the farmer left, probably to get a shovel, I got up and headed toward the house of Frank Colbert. You remember him, Nigel. He was one of the underground men who helped us with our mission. I almost bled to death before I got there."

Fister leaned back in his chair, stretched out his long legs, and crossed one ankle over the other. "Colbert patched me up the best he could and hid me away. I stayed there until after Christmas, regaining my strength. When more Germans were transferred into the area, Colbert and his group moved me to a hiding place just outside of Paris. Later I was smuggled to Spain and finally given over to a group of merchant seamen. They got me on a ship bound for America. When I arrived in New York, I came straight to Washington and checked in with the embassy."

"Amazing," Meeker said. "Did the Nazis ever get close to capturing you during your months behind lines?"

"A couple of times. I had to kill two Gestapo agents with my bare hands," Fister bragged. "I thought I was a goner when some lads spotted me. But they were soft; they didn't offer much of a fight."

"When did you get to Washington?" Andrews asked.

"About three weeks ago. I had my injuries checked out at Walter Reed Hospital and have been in debriefings ever since I was released. Hopefully what I saw will help us knock out some Jerry installations. When I get back to England, I'll receive my promotion, working for the high command. So I'll be dealing with Monty and Ike on a regular basis."

"That's quite an honor," Meeker said. "You'll soon know more about the war and Allied plans than even Roosevelt and Churchill."

Fister grinned. "I doubt that. But I will be in a position to give a regular soldier's viewpoint before we charge off into battles. Maybe that will help us save a few chaps like Nigel here. If so, I will have done my part."

The colonel leaned farther forward, his eyes all but staring through Meeker. "I do hope in the next few weeks you'll make time to show me some of the sights in this beautiful city. I've heard so much about Washington over the years and would love to have someone like you be my guide."

Meeker nodded, her palms clammy. "Perhaps. But only if it doesn't interfere with my work for the president."

An astonished look framed the Brit's sparkling eyes. "You

mean Mr. Roosevelt?"

"Yes. I'm his special assistant and we're in the middle of an important assignment right now." She glanced at her wristwatch and noticed the time. "As a matter of fact, I need to check in with my partner now. So if you'll excuse me, I must be heading out." She stood, and the two men followed suit.

At the door, Fister extended his hand. "I trust we will meet again and you can show me your city."

"If time allows."

"How can I reach you?"

"Just call the White House." She turned to Andrews. "Nigel, thank you for your time, and I do hope you get back to Becky very soon. I too pray we will find a way to end this war, sacrificing as few lives as possible." She flashed a smile at each of them. "Good night, gentlemen." She headed to the door. After opening it, she turned and found Fister close behind her. "Welcome back from the dead, Colonel."

Without waiting for a response, she hurried down the hall to the front door. As she drove her yellow Packard toward home, though she was completely alone, she still felt Reggie Fister's hand touching hers. It was too soon to determine if that was a good thing or the right temptation at the wrong time.

CHAPTER 16

Monday, March 9, 1942
Germantown, New York

Helen Meeker studied the traffic on Ivy Street from the passenger side of the 1935 Dodge panel truck. The cold day felt more like winter than spring, so she appreciated the warmth of the standard-issue blue-gray Red Cross uniform, with its wool gabardine jacket, skirt, coat, and cap—though it was hardly the usual attire for a president's assistant.

"How do I look?" she asked her partner.

Reese pointed at the emblem on her jacket sleeve. "Just like a real member of the Red Cross."

"As do you."

He sighed. "I still wish I could wear my marine uniform."

"I'm sorry J. Edgar blocked you from that. But these clothes will work better today. We don't want anyone who might be watching the Shellmeyer home to know who we really are."

"I suppose you're right," he muttered as he parked the distinctly marked vehicle used by the Red Cross for blood drives. "But this is not one of my favorite covers."

Meeker didn't dignify his complaint with a response. "You take this side of the street; I'll take the far side. Knock on a few doors and say you're looking for donations. If they seem agreeable, ask if you can come in out of the cold to explain the importance of our program. Then it won't seem strange when I gain entry to the Shellmeyer house. Assuming I do."

"Got it."

They stepped out of the truck.

"Honk when you need me to end my cold day of humiliation."

Meeker rolled her eyes at him.

Reese strolled up the sidewalk to a home, knocked on the door, and went into his spiel. Assured he was going to play his role like a pro, Meeker crossed to the other side of the street. For an hour and a half, she worked her way toward the Shellmeyers' modest two-story white clapboard house. During that time she met nine lonely housewives, four children, and an old maid, and gathered eighteen dollars in donations.

Smoothing her coat, she took a deep breath and strolled up the walk toward her real objective. After climbing three steps, she crossed the covered porch to the front door. She twisted the bell.

A few moments later, a too-thin woman, with pale skin and sunken deep-blue eyes, opened the door. In spite of her gaunt appearance, Meeker recognized Virginia Shellmeyer from the pictures she'd seen in the files. The woman looked sadder than anyone she'd ever seen.

"May I help you?" she asked in a lifeless voice.

Meeker began her rehearsed lines. "I'm with the Red Cross, and we're seeking donations to better serve our soldiers, both here and overseas."

"I'm sorry," the woman mumbled. "We have no extra money. The only reason we have a roof over our heads is that my brother loaned us one of his rental houses."

As Mrs. Shellmeyer stepped back and began to close the door, Meeker hurriedly added, "I understand that, and I sympathize with you. But I've been on the streets most of the morning, and I'm really cold. Would you perhaps have a cup of coffee you could share with me? I'll be happy to pay for it."

"All right," came the weary response. "That's the least I can do."

As the door swung open, Meeker scooted inside. After closing and latching the entry, her host said, "Let me take you back to the kitchen. I have some coffee on the stove."

"Mrs. Shellmeyer," Meeker cut in, "I don't really need the coffee. And I'm not with the Red Cross."

What little color there was in Mrs. Shellmeyer's face drained away.

"I'm working with the FBI and the office of the president. And though I might be one of the few, I don't believe your husband is guilty."

She glanced out the window. "You shouldn't be here," she whispered. "If they see you, they'll …" Her voice trailed off as she stared at the street.

"What will they do?"

"Nothing. You need to go."

Meeker moved into her hostess's line of vision and stared into the woman's frightened eyes. "Mrs. Shellmeyer, I am absolutely certain your husband is not a spy."

"You shouldn't say such things," she pleaded. "Now, please leave before they find out you're here."

"Who are they?"

"I don't know," she whined, wringing her hands. "I've never met them face-to-face. But they told me they're watching our every move."

"How did they tell you?"

"Through phone calls and letters. And I know it's true. I can feel their eyes on me. They can hear what we're saying right now. They might even know what we're thinking." She shuddered.

Meeker looked toward the hall and into the dining room. Though convinced that no one was in earshot, she whispered, "What does Zion mean?"

Mrs. Shellmeyer's face registered surprise at the question. "It's heaven."

"I know that. But what did your husband's prayer at the graveside mean?"

"I have no idea." The woman sobbed. "He was grief-struck. He probably didn't know what he was saying."

Meeker placed her hand on the woman's arm. "What happened to your daughter?"

She wiped a tear from her cheek with the back of her hand. "We were on vacation. Ellen disappeared from her bed, and Will went out to find her. He was gone almost all day. When he came back, he told me she'd been swimming in the ocean and a shark attacked her."

"Did you see her body?"

She shook her head. "Will said I shouldn't because it was so mangled. He didn't want me to remember her that way."

"Did you have any idea that he was spying?"

"No. And I still say he couldn't be a Nazi spy. He loved America. That's why we were on that vacation. He had some kind of important news he wanted to share with a man who was with some government group. They'd gone to college together." A sudden look of fright crossed her face. "I shouldn't have said that. Will made me promise never to tell anyone."

"It's all right. I'm here to help." Meeker patted the woman's trembling shoulder. "Can you tell me where this meeting was supposed to take place?"

"I don't know. I guess somewhere in Gulfport, Mississippi, since that's where we went. But Ellen died before the meeting could take place."

Meeker glanced out the front window. Seeing no activity on the street, she continued. "Who were the two men at the cemetery with you?"

"They were from the funeral home in Gulfport. They led us to that place in Georgia."

"Did you talk to them?"

"No," she all but whispered. "They rode in a different car."

"Did you get their names?"

Mrs. Shellmeyer shook her head. "Sorry."

"What did they look like?"

"They were probably in their thirties, well dressed, pretty big. I remember thinking they looked like they could have played football or maybe boxed." She paused. "One of them had an ear that looked kind of beaten up, like a fighter's. And he had a scar under his right ... no, wait, his left eye."

"Hair color?"

"Dirty blond."

"Any details on the other one?"

She shifted her gaze to the far wall. "He had kind of a square jaw, and a mole above his dark eyes. When he reached out to grab Ellen's coffin, I saw some kind of tattoo on his left wrist."

"A tattoo of what?"

"It was barely visible beneath the sleeve of his shirt. It might have been an arrowhead. I'm not sure."

"Thank you. You've been a big help."

"With what?" Shellmeyer's tone turned bitter. "Making my husband look even more guilty?" She glanced out the window. "Or maybe the government thinks I'm a spy too."

"I don't believe either one of you could be guilty of that. And I'm hoping to be able to prove that."

Mrs. Shellmeyer shot her a glare. "Will is going to die in a week."

"I know. But have faith."

"Faith in what?"

Meeker wished she had an answer.

CHAPTER 17

Helen Meeker hit a half dozen more homes before she headed back to the truck and blew the horn. Within a minute Reece was back behind the wheel and had the Dodge pointed south. Two miles down the road, he'd nursed the panel truck up to fifty. Apparently he couldn't wait to get back to New York, give the old vehicle and uniforms back to the Red Cross, and once again don the more familiar role and appearance of an FBI agent.

"Mrs. Shellmeyer believes her daughter is dead," Meeker announced.

"Did you tell her any different?" Reese asked, keeping his eyes on the road.

"No. I couldn't get her hopes up when we aren't sure where the kid is … or if she really is alive."

"What does she think about her husband being a spy?"

"She doesn't buy that. And she doesn't seem to know why he confessed. But there was something she said that might point us in the right direction." Meeker stared out the window at the passing New York countryside.

"You going to fill me in or not?"

She turned back to face him. "Have you come across anything in Shellmeyer's logbook that indicates he planned on meeting someone in Gulfport?"

He shook his head. "There's absolutely nothing about that whole week in the book. This guy went into great detail on almost every facet of his life before Gulfport, but he barely noted anything about the trip or the days leading up to his arrest."

Meeker sighed. "His wife told me he was meeting someone down there, an old college friend, and he was going to give him some kind of information the US government would be interested in."

"He did mention some friends in the book. I could go back through those names and see if any of them went to college with him and have a connection to Gulfport."

"It's about all we have to go on." She paused for a moment and admired Reese's square jaw and rugged good looks, but stopped short when her perusal morphed into a comparison of Reese and Fister. She'd no more than thought of the Scotsman when the man she was admiring said his name.

"So, what were you able to find out about Reggie Fister?"

"Oh, not much," she said, feigning disinterest.

"Surely you picked up some details. Give it to me like an agent would."

"All right. He's … interesting. Very smooth and charming. He's got those English manners that most men on this side of the pond don't have." She shrugged. "I guess he's the kind of guy a lot of girls could fall for."

Reese smiled. "So you fell for him. It's that stupid accent, isn't it? "

"No," she shot back. "You asked me about him, and I gave you a report. That's all!"

He laughed. "He has you under his spell." His tone took on an edge of sarcasm. "Men in uniform always get attention."

"There you go again, feeling sorry for yourself," Meeker jabbed. "You're doing just as much for your country right now as any of those boys in the military. Besides, you look pretty dapper in that uniform you're wearing."

"Yeah, sure," he grumbled.

As the old truck approached a sharp curve, Reese eased off the gas and slipped his foot over to the brake. But the truck did not slow down.

"Take it easy," Meeker suggested. "Just because you're mad, you don't need to be playing around."

"I'm not." Jamming the clutch to the floor, Reese shifted into second. The gears screamed. The truck lurched and groaned. It slowed a bit, but not enough to safely maneuver the upcoming bend in the highway.

"What's going on?" Meeker shouted.

"No brakes!" Reese gripped the wheel with both hands and pulled hard to the right.

Just ahead, a two-ton milk truck came around the curve. With only one lane at his disposal, Reese gave the emergency brake a hard pull. Nothing happened.

"Hang on," Reece hollered. "We may need some of that Red Cross blood soon," he muttered through gritted teeth.

As Meeker braced herself against the dashboard, the panel truck's right tires dropped off the pavement and onto the grassy shoulder. A hundred feet after leaving the asphalt, the front tire found a large pothole.

The hole pulled both of the front wheels sharply to the right, pushing the truck off the road and toward the woods. Meeker covered her face with her arms and pushed her feet into the floorboard. Reese, still fighting the steering wheel, tried one final time to change the truck's course. He failed.

The old Dodge skimmed a century-old oak with the driver's side fender, then careened into an impressive maple on the right side of the car. The maple pushed the truck down a steep draw. The passenger-side tires left the ground, and the truck rolled over onto its side.

Meeker was thrown on top of Reese as the vehicle skidded another fifty yards. He threw his right arm around her in a protective gesture that did little to shield her from the glass that shot onto them as a tree limb broke the truck's windshield.

"You all right?" he asked when the wild ride finally came to an end.

"I'm fine." Meeker pushed off her partner and glanced through what was left of the front glass. She was bruised and shaken, but nothing felt broken.

"Cover your face," Reese ordered as he aimed his shoes at what was left of the windshield. "If I kick out the remaining glass, we can get out through there."

It took three strong kicks for him to accomplish his mission. After he did, Meeker pulled herself around the steering wheel and fell out onto the bank of a slow-moving creek. She had just managed to stand when Reese stepped out of the cab.

"What happened?" she asked.

"I'd say you got us a bum truck," he snapped back.

After she'd regained her equilibrium, Meeker walked around the front of the vehicle. With the truck lying on its side, she could easily study the undercarriage.

"Virginia Shellmeyer was right," she announced as Reese joined her.

"About what?"

"She said someone was watching her and could hear everything we were saying."

Reese frowned. "And you believe her?"

Meeker moved to the back of the vehicle and pointed to a spot near the rear passenger tire. "Tell me what you see."

Reese sucked in a breath. "The line's been cut."

"So has the emergency-brake cable."

"Who would do that to a Red Cross truck?"

Meeker thought back to her meeting with Mrs. Shellmeyer. She had seen no one, and the free manner in which the woman spoke surely meant they were alone. So how had their identity been revealed?

"There must be bugs in the house," she said.

Reese rubbed his jaw. "Do you think this was a warning? Or was it meant to kill us?"

The words had no sooner left his lips than a shot rang out,

the bullet striking the tire just above Meeker's head. Three more volleys followed. She fell to the ground and crawled around the truck. Reese rolled through the grass and joined her a second later.

"Does that answer your question?" Meeker whispered.

CHAPTER 18

Helen Meeker peeked around the edge of the upturned panel truck and toward a stand of woods on a hill from where the shots had come. She could see no one. Another round bounced off the vehicle's rear bumper, causing her to duck back.

"What do you think?" Reese asked.

"I figure there's only one of them. If there were more, we would've been peppered with firepower. Where's your gun?"

"In the cab of the truck."

"Mine too. In my handbag."

Four more shots rang out, all hitting the truck's underbelly.

"Why is he wasting bullets?" Meeker asked. "He can't see us."

Reese crawled up toward the front of the vehicle and crouched behind the hood. "He's going for the gas tank."

"Can he blow us up?"

He shrugged. "That works pretty well in Hollywood movies,

but the odds are a bit longer in real life. Still, he could get lucky."

"I was too close to an explosion once already this week. I don't need more stitches in my arm."

Ducking down, Reese slid into the truck's cab. The attacker ripped off five more rounds. Reese rolled back out onto the ground, Meeker's purse and his gun in his hands, and crawled to where she was sitting, her back pinned against the vehicle's roof.

"He's on the move," she told Reese as he sat beside her.

"How do you know?"

"The angle of the shots is changing. He appears to be heading south. We're going to be sitting ducks within a minute or so if we don't get up that hill and into those woods."

Reese grimaced. "Do you smell what I smell?"

Meeker took a sniff. "Gas."

"The tank is leaking. He must have hit his target at least once. Do you have any matches in your purse?"

"Yes."

"Give them to me. I'm going to start a fire. I'm betting that when he sees the smoke and flames, he'll move back to get farther away from the truck. That should give us a few seconds to make our get-away."

After digging out the matchbook and handing it to Reese, Meeker glanced toward the trees. "Looks to be about thirty yards to the woods. Bet I can beat you there."

"You're on." He crawled to the rear of the truck and fell to his stomach about three feet from a puddle of gas. After placing his gun on the ground, he pulled out a match and struck it against a nearby stone. When it flamed, he tossed it toward the puddle. It went out before it landed. As he pulled out a second match, two shots hit the dirt just in front of his head.

"I could use some help," he barked.

Meeker aimed her Colt into the woods and squeezed off four quick rounds. Reese lit the second match and held it against the cover until the cardboard caught on fire. Within seconds the rest of the book's matches sparked. Rising to his knees, he tossed the flaming box toward the puddle. It landed dead center. In one fluid movement, he rolled over, grabbed his gun, fired two quick rounds, and headed toward the woods.

After pulling her trigger one more time to give Reese a bit of cover, Meeker raced toward the trees. Two shots rang out from behind her, peppering the hillside to her left. A second later she heard the roar of the gas exploding. From the corner of her eye she watched the back of the truck lift off the ground and twist to the side.

"Keep moving," Reese called out.

She didn't need his order. She wasn't about to stop for anything or anyone.

Finally, she dove into the wooded area and behind a tree, her partner a split second behind.

"Told you I'd beat you," she taunted as she opened her purse and reloaded her weapon.

"You cheated," he grumbled. "You started before I did."

"A victory is a victory. So, what do you suggest now?"

"The highway should be about a hundred yards through these woods. We should be able to flag down a ride."

After putting her gun in her purse, she rose to her feet and moved deeper into the woods. Reese was with her step for step. It took them five minutes to push through the timber and make it back to the two-lane highway.

Looking down the road, Meeker noted a rusty Model AA truck headed their way. As Reese slid his firearm inside his jacket, she stepped out onto the highway and waved to the driver. The truck came to a stop.

"Can we help you folks?" a teenage girl asked from the passenger-side window. The fresh-faced redhead gave Reese a coy smile.

Meeker nodded. "We had some car trouble back a spell and need a lift to the nearest town."

On the far side of the decade-old, ton-and-a-half vehicle, the driver's door creaked open. A middle-aged man wearing bib overalls got out and moved around the front of the truck to greet them.

"My name's David Sellers. I own a farm about ten miles back. Me, the wife, and my daughter are taking a few hogs to town." He eyed the emblems on the ragged-looking pair's sleeves. "You two with the Red Cross?"

"You have a good eye," Reese said.

Sellers gave them a big grin. "Well, then, you folks are welcome to jump in with us. The cab's full, so you'll have to ride in back with the hogs."

"Beggars can't be choosers," Reese quipped.

"Just climb in over the back gate. Those hogs are pretty big, but they won't hurt you."

As they got to the rear of the old truck, Reese grabbed

Meeker's waist and lifted her until her feet touched the bottom the back gate. As she climbed over the three wooden rails to the top, she lost her grip and fell onto one of the hogs. The black-and-white beast squealed and lurched forward, then turned around and nosed the intruder's lips. Grabbing the side of the truck, Meeker pulled herself upright, wiped her mouth with her sleeve, whirled, and glared at the pig. Reese snickered. She shot him a scorching glare too.

After climbing over the gate and dropping gracefully into the back of the truck's bed, Reese grinned. "I think he likes you. And I bet he has the same delicate charm and manners as Reggie." He laughed. "Can't say you didn't bring home the bacon."

As Sellers put the truck into gear and it eased back on the road, Meeker snarled at her partner. He laughed and pointed to her skirt. "I hope that's just mud."

She looked at her soiled skirt. "Doesn't matter now. The uniform did its job." She glanced between the slats at a car that was following about a hundred yards behind them. "Do you suppose that's the guy who tried to plug us?"

He glanced back. "No way to tell. Just to be safe, let's keep hunkered down where he can't see us."

Holding on to the railing for balance, Meeker studied the blue sedan behind them. "Henry, how many states do you think have towns named Zion?"

He shrugged. "Scores, probably."

"Have the folks at your office find all of them, starting with those in the South. My gut tells me Ellen Shellmeyer might be in one of them."

He nodded. "I can send out an alert to our people in each state where there's a Zion. But I'll need a photo of the girl."

Meeker pushed her grunting new admirer with the heel of her pump. "I'm sure her school in Newport has one. We could probably get hold of a copy of last year's school annual."

Reese groaned. "And while I'm hopping all over the country, what will you be doing with your time?"

She fluttered her lashes. "Why, I'll be working for the president, of course."

"Doing what?"

She shrugged. "I'm having dinner with Reggie Fister tomorrow night."

Reese frowned. "I have a suggestion."

"What's that?"

"Take the pig along."

CHAPTER 19

Tuesday, March 10, 1942
Washington, DC

Helen Meeker chose a simple purple blouse, gray jacket, and matching skirt for her dinner engagement with Reggie Fister. After dressing, she drove her Packard to the Royal Hotel. He was waiting on the sidewalk just outside the ornate, well-lit entry, dressed in a charcoal tweed suit, white shirt, and dark tie. He looked dashing, to say the least.

During the ten-minute drive to Rigatti's Café, one of the city's popular hot spots, Reggie filled the car with a string of compliments about everything from the shape of Meeker's ankles to the color of her eyes. If the trip had taken any longer, he might have mentioned an area that would have required her to slap him.

Once inside the restaurant, they sat at a corner table near the piano. He ate spaghetti, while she opted for a salad. Their dinner conversation centered on what Fister had observed during his last two days in Washington. After the meal, the waiter removed their empty plates and brought two steaming mugs of coffee.

"I'm glad you're enjoying our city," Meeker said as she sipped her hot brew. "Did your guides tell you that the British Army once burned it to the ground?"

Fister frowned. "That was not one of our better moves."

She smiled. "If you'd been serving in the military then, would you have followed those orders?"

"I'm a military man." He shrugged. "That's what we do. Our obligations are first and foremost to our duties. I don't believe I have ever disobeyed an order."

"I see." Meeker arched an eyebrow.

"However," he added quickly, "if you had lived then and we had met, I would likely have disregarded that one. I could not have left such a beautiful woman homeless, no matter what my superiors wanted me to do."

She smiled. "Of all your lines tonight, that one might well be the worst."

Fister gave her a sly grin, then took her hand in his. "To be honest, I didn't actually spend much time touring the city the past two days."

"Really?"

"I spent most of that time finding out more about you."

She was a little taken aback. What did he mean? And what kind of information did he uncover? She didn't care for folks snooping into her personal life.

He patted her hand and flashed his perfect teeth. "Don't get too concerned. It's not the way it sounds. The fact is, I realized the moment we met that I'd never known anyone like you."

"A lot of people say that. And they don't always mean it as a good thing." In spite of her usually reticent nature, she felt almost pleased that this handsome soldier knew so much about her. Part of her longed to tell him more.

He caressed her fingers. "The way you carry yourself is almost regal. Your beauty is addicting. Your intelligence and wit are beyond any I have ever known in the lassies back home. I could study you for the next year and never grow bored." He leaned closer. "I think of you as a flower that is ever in bloom."

Her cheeks felt hot. "Like flowers, I tend to wilt from time to time. You should have seen me yesterday."

"I'm not only impressed by your beauty. Your work amazes me too. Scotland Yard could use someone like you."

"Not if their rules are like those at the FBI. It's totally a boys' club."

Ignoring her quip, Fister gazed into her eyes. "I was especially fascinated by the case I read about where you found that little girl and reunited her with her parents. You uncovered clues that everyone else missed. That was quite impressive."

Meeker nodded. "That investigation also led to my reuniting with my sister. Alison has brought a great deal of joy to my life. When this terrible war is over, I hope I can get to know her even better."

"Is she still in Chicago?"

"No. She's at a small college in Arkansas. She's a bright girl, and I want her to reach her potential. This country can't remain a man's world forever. Maybe she can be one of those who changes that."

"Are you paying for her education?"

She shrugged. "I have more than enough to do that."

"Oh, that's right. Your family had some money."

She felt her heart skip a beat, and she drew her brows together. "Just how much research did you do on me?"

He grinned. "I know how much you weighed at birth."

"I'm flattered. At least, I think I am."

The smile left his lips. "I'm sorry if I've made you uncomfortable." He pulled back his hand and set his elbows on the cloth-covered table. "You must understand. I am military through and through, and I have a background in intelligence. When I find an objective, I learn everything I can to better prepare me to achieve my goals."

"And am I part of a campaign? One of your goals?"

A bit of the sparkle returned to his eyes. "That doesn't sound like what I meant, but it might well be true. I have only a few weeks here before I go back to England, which means a very short time to convince you that your life cannot be complete without having me in it."

She shook her head, her emotions a jumble of curiosity and apprehension. "Reggie, we just met. I don't know how things work in England, but they don't move that quickly here—at least not with me."

He touched her arm. "Helen, there is a war on. Thousands die every day. We no longer measure our lives in years. We have to think in moments." He leaned across the table and allowed his lips to gently brush hers. "The moments I have I want to spend with you. You might well be the last woman I hold and the only woman I ever truly come to love."

As he sat back in his chair, his kiss stayed with her, and a fog, deeper than any that had ever invaded London, pushed into her mind. This man was good-looking, charming, and heroic. The kind of man who could sweep any woman off her feet. That made him not only desirable but dangerous.

His voice pulled her attention back from the cacophony of longing and warning sirens going off in her brain. "I'm glad you weren't hurt yesterday."

"Excuse me?"

He smiled. "When you were in New York."

Her breath caught in her throat. "How did you know I was in New York yesterday?"

"I called the White House to try to reach you. The woman who was taking your calls told me."

"Oh." Feeling uncomfortable, she glanced at her watch. "I hate to break up this incredible evening, but it's time for me to go."

"So soon? I was hoping we could go dancing."

"Not tonight." She rose from her seat. "I have an early day tomorrow."

He followed her to the door. No more words were exchanged until they got into her car and she drove back onto the street.

"I'm not sure how much time I have left in this country," he said in a somber tone. "I have some duties coming up that will require my full attention. But I would love to monopolize your time for the next few weeks."

"That's sweet. But I have an important job too. What I'm working on now might mean the difference between life and death for several people."

"Couldn't someone else handle it?"

"Not as well as I can."

"Are you sure about that?"

"Yes, I am."

From the corner of her eye, she saw him grin. "Maybe I could talk to the president and convince him how important it would be, to both me and Britain, to have you by my side while I'm in the States."

"Don't you dare," she snapped without taking her eyes off the road. "My work is important, so don't try to get in the way of it."

He paused. "May I ask what is so important about your current case?"

"No, Reggie, you can't. I'm not at liberty to talk about it, not even with my sister."

"I see." Meeker detected genuine sadness in his tone. "You don't trust me."

"That's not it," she assured him.

"Perhaps, with my experience and training, I might be able to help."

"If something comes up where I need you, I'll call you."

As they waited at a red light, she looked over to Fister. His face was drawn and tight, and his eyes were locked on the road ahead. "Reggie, I can't change what I do or who I am."

He nodded. "I understand. But please tell me you are safe. You're not doing anything that might put you in harm's way, are you?"

The light changed, and she pulled the Packard forward. After going through two shifts, she finally answered. "If you've done your research, you know I don't take the easy, safe route."

"And is your sister safe too?"

"What do you mean?"

"Can you be sure that what you're doing is not putting her in danger?"

She had never considered that. But the odds were long against anything she was involved in affecting Alison. Her sister was a long way from DC.

"All my sister has to worry about is making sure the guys in Arkadelphia don't fall all over each other while lining up for dates with her."

He laughed. "Then she must be as beautiful as you are."

Meeker pulled up in front of his hotel, put the car in neutral, and set the brake. She got out and walked her date to the door. "Thanks for the nice evening ... and for your concern."

His arms wrapped around her waist and he drew her close. With their lips just inches apart, he whispered, "I could give you a life where you wouldn't have any risks ... unless you consider loving me a risk." He covered her mouth with his and kissed her hard and long. The kiss took her breath away and left her knees wobbly. When he finally pulled back, she felt lightheaded.

After letting her slowly slide from his arms, he whispered, "Call me when you're free."

She watched him enter the hotel's revolving door before turning on her heels and hurrying back to her car. She sat in the driver's seat for a few moments, allowing her heart to slow, then released the brake and put the car into first gear.

A hundred feet or so down the street, she felt something cold on the back of her neck. "Keep going until I say to stop," a deep voice whispered. "And don't even think about calling out for help."

CHAPTER 20

Helen Meeker drove four blocks before her uninvited passenger in the sedan's rear seat removed the gun barrel from the back of her neck. "Where are we going?"

"Park by the Lincoln Memorial. And just because I no longer have my gun against your neck, that doesn't mean you're safe. There are a lot of ways to kill someone, and my training has taught me most of them."

The man's voice sounded familiar. She'd heard it recently but couldn't place where. She glanced in the rearview mirror, but the hat pulled low over his eyes kept her from seeing his face.

A quiet five minutes passed before she pulled into a parking place in the nearly vacant lot beside the memorial. She set the brake, turned off the key, and waited for the intruder to give her further instructions.

"Get out of the car, and leave your purse here. I'm sure you have a gun in there, and I don't want to have to use mine. Do you understand?"

"Yes." She lifted the door handle and stepped out into the cool, damp air. As she waited for further instructions, she found herself wishing she'd opted to dance the night away with Reggie Fister. Perhaps, if he hadn't pushed the romance angle so hard, she would have. But that scared her even more than having a stranger hijack her car.

"Walk up to the top step," he ordered as he closed the Packard's back door. "And don't turn around. I'll be right behind you."

It took Meeker just over two minutes to climb the fifty-seven steps leading up to the top level of the memorial. When she reached the landing, she turned to face the man calling the shots. Now face-to-face, she recognized him immediately. "Nigel?"

"That's right." The corporal was dressed in civilian clothing, and she didn't see a gun anywhere.

"What's this all about?"

"I'm not here to hurt you," he said, no longer trying to disguise his voice. "I just needed to get you alone so I could tell you something. Can we sit here on the steps?"

"All right." Smoothing her skirt, she took a seat on the top stair. He took a position about a foot to her right. "You didn't have to kidnap me just to talk."

"Sorry about the tough-guy act. But I don't have Reggie's confidence or charm." Andrews placed his hands on his knees and stared off into the distance. "How old is this memorial?"

"Two decades."

"Your country is very young."

"Compared to Europe, yes."

He silently laid his head on his arms.

"What's going on with you? I know you're disillusioned about the war and I understand how you feel about those who are sending men off to die. But what you did tonight doesn't fit your profile. You're a gentleman, with ideals and manners."

"I'm also a man who desperately wants peace." He lifted his face from his arms. "I was going to be a pastor. Did you know that? I wanted to teach men how to love one another. But my country turned me into a killing machine. I hate what I've become. And I hate the roll of playing the hero." He sighed. "I even hate that Reggie is alive, because it means he'll get the opportunity to kill even more men."

"That's a lot of hatred for someone who once considered going into the pastorate."

"I also hate that you're seeing him. You'll fall under his spell, just like everyone. It seems no woman can resist him."

Meeker smiled. "Is that what this is all about? Nigel, I don't know what he's told you, but I'm not the type of girl to get serious in a hurry."

"Even my Becky couldn't resist his charms," Andrews lamented. "The moment she met him, her feelings for me cooled."

"It was likely just a schoolgirl crush," Meeker assured him. "All women get those. It's nothing to worry about. They don't last."

"It doesn't matter. What's really wrong is that Reggie came

back. I was there. He was surrounded by Germans. None of us should have survived."

"Miracles happen," Meeker assured him. "Sometimes God steps in and bends all logic."

"That's the only explanation that almost makes sense."

Meeker studied the man's face. He was obviously confused and deeply troubled.

"Have you ever had someone take a shot at you?"

"Yes." As a matter of fact, it had happened much more recently than she wanted to reveal.

"What happens when folks are laying down fire all around you?"

"Well …" She gave the question serious thought. "Dirt kicks up. Stuff around me gets hit. I can even hear bullets fly past my head."

"None of that happened the night we got away in France. Except for Homes, none of us was hit, even though scores of Germans were shooting at us. I saw the guns flaming in the woods, and I heard the shots echoing all around me. But when I got to thinking about it last night, I realized that none of the rounds hit the ground around me. And there wasn't a single bullet hole in the airplane. There should have been hundreds."

His observation made sense. There probably should have been at least some damage and probably more casualties.

He locked eyes with her. "If Reggie's heroics had drawn the fire away from us, he should have been hit him numerous times. Yet he only took three bullets. No one is that bad a shot."

"What are you suggesting?"

"I don't know. But Reggie shouldn't be alive, and neither should the rest of us. And that plane should never have gotten off the ground. Those Germans had to be there all the time, just waiting for us. So why couldn't they stop us?"

He posed an excellent question. Meeker wondered why no one had asked it before.

Andrews stood and shoved his hands into his pockets. "Let's go back to your car. There's something there I need you to look at."

Meeker followed him to the Packard. He opened the back door and pulled out a folder, then slid into the front seat. She followed his lead and took her position behind the wheel.

"Could you turn on the dome light?" he asked.

Meeker flipped the switch.

"These are Reggie's medical files. I lifted them from the embassy. I want you to glance over them."

Meeker took the papers and skimmed through the reports of the colonel's evaluation at Walter Reed. She observed the diagrams of his three bullet wounds, studied a photo taken of the entry and exit locations of those rounds, read over the notes about his weight, height, and general health, then closed the file and handed it back to Andrews. "What did you want me to see?"

"The wounds. They were all flesh wounds."

"That's why he survived. If they'd been serious, he would have died."

"Wounds like his would have been made by small-caliber weapons. This was war, not a bird shoot."

Meeker traced her lips with her right index finger, intrigued by where this was leading.

"I'm being sent back to England tomorrow," Andrews said. "No one told me why. But Reggie will be taking my place as Churchill's personal guard." He looked her in the eye. "Don't trust him, Helen."

Before she could offer a response, Andrews pulled up on the car's handle and stepped outside. Then he leaned back in. "Do you believe in ghosts?"

"No."

"Neither do I. And I don't believe in miracles either." He shut the door and walked off.

When Andrews was beyond her sight, Meeker restarted her car and drove back across town to her apartment, trying to make sense of what she'd just seen and heard.

As she unlocked her front door, she heard her phone ringing. She rushed to the bedroom and grabbed the receiver. "This is Helen Meeker."

"You're finally home," Fister said. "I've called several times."

"I had some ... work to do. What's up?"

"I don't know if I told you this, but I had a wonderful time tonight."

"I think you hinted at that when we said good night."

"I suppose I did." He laughed. "But that's not the only reason I called. I have something serious to tell you, and it must stay between us, at least for the moment."

"What's that?"

"I was given some reports this evening from British

126

Intelligence, and they indicate that Nigel Andrews might be working for the Nazis."

"Really?"

"I always pegged him as a great lad. But the entire time we were in France I sensed that one of my men was not on the up-and-up."

"What gave you that impression?"

"I found notes that had been dropped along a road that gave the location of a secret base in Wales."

"Is that it?"

"No. I got word last week that Colbert, a man who worked with us, was discovered and killed by the Nazis. Someone in our group must have blown his cover."

"That seems like pretty weak logic to me."

"There's more. The plane that took my boys home made it off the ground without having a single bullet strike it. I have to wonder if the attack was staged. They killed one of us just to make it look good. But they needed to make sure Nigel got back to England so he could keep feeding them information. And his hero stature, along with his new assignments, give him access to plenty of information the Germans could use against us."

His conclusions didn't really add up, not after what Nigel had told her. But she didn't reveal her thoughts to him.

"If that's true, I wasn't a hero after all. I didn't need to hold off the Germans. They would have let me get on the plane too."

"Well, that does explain a lot about the miracle."

"Miracle?"

"Never mind." She sighed. "You sleep well, Reggie."

"You too, Helen. And please, stay away from Nigel. Whatever he tells you, don't believe it."

After placing the receiver back into the cradle, Meeker crossed the room and snapped the lock on her door. Who was yanking her string? Was it the recognized hero, or the man who had served as his stand-in? She wouldn't rest well until she knew.

CHAPTER 21

Wednesday, March 11, 1942
United States Federal Penitentiary
Lewisburg, Pennsylvania

While Reese stayed in Washington to put his efforts into finding out whether Ellen Shellmeyer was alive, and if so, where she was being held, Helen Meeker drove her yellow Packard to the prison where Wilbur Shellmeyer awaited death. After being processed, she was ushered into Warden Scott Dennis's office and given a seat across from the prison official's desk.

"Shellmeyer is not a typical guest for us," the middle-aged man explained. Smoothing his salt-and-pepper hair, he looked out into the prison yard. Though of average height and build, Dennis carried himself with an authority that would likely have intimidated most prisoners. His voice was deep and his dark eyes intense. "We usually cater to the organized crime lord types. I'm not used to someone as gentle and unassuming as Shellmeyer.

He seems to me like a sad man who has given up on life."

Meeker smoothed her black jacket where it met her fitted gray wool skirt. "I think I might know the reason for that."

Dennis turned back to face his guest. "Care to share it?"

"Not at this time. But perhaps after I talk to him."

He nodded. "He's waiting for you in a room right off my office. Since he's shackled, you should be safe alone with him."

Meeker rose. "Thank you."

"Follow me." He led her out a side door, down a long hallway, and to a door where one prison guard stood vigil. Seeing the warden, the tall, powerfully built man stepped aside. With a turn of a knob, the door opened into a sterile, fifteen-foot room containing only a table and four chairs. A thin, tired-looking man in a gray shirt sat at the far end of the table. His blond hair was cropped short, and dark circles drooped beneath his light-blue eyes.

"Wilbur," the warden said, "this is Miss Helen Meeker. She's from the office of the president. She wants to ask you a few questions, and I have agreed to allow her to be alone with you. I trust you will show her the respect she deserves."

As the warden left the room and closed the door, Shellmeyer's eyes remained on Meeker. She took a seat to his right, set her purse on the floor beside her, and forced a smile. He didn't respond.

"Should I call you Wilbur? Or do you prefer Reverend Shellmeyer?"

"It doesn't matter." His tone signaled an overriding sense of defeat.

"Okay, Wilbur. I know you didn't spy on the United States. I believe you're innocent. And I think you're willing to die for something you didn't do in order to protect someone you love."

His eyes grew wide. "I gave them the notes and photos. I told them what I did."

She reached into her purse and pulled out a notepad. After flipping through several pages, she looked back to him. "On the dates you were supposedly spying, you were actually officiating at weddings or funerals, conducting conferences, or preaching."

"You must be mistaken," he whispered.

"So which is wrong? Your church records or the reports you gave to the FBI?"

"I don't know. But I did what I said I did, and I'm going to pay for it with my life next week."

"You can certainly do that if you want to. But you aren't dying because you were a spy. You're dying because you're protecting someone. So who's really working for the Nazis? Is it your wife?"

"No," he shot back, exhibiting passion for the first time. "Virginia knew nothing."

"I believe you. I've met her, and she's not cut out for that kind of work. Which leads me to consider another option."

"Why can't you just believe I did it and let it go?" he begged.

"If you hadn't confessed, there isn't a court in this country that would convict you. But no one looked closely enough at the evidence to realize you were taking the fall for someone else."

"No," he moaned. "I did it."

"I've been to your daughter's grave, Wilbur."

His face registered shock.

"Now, tell me this. What did you mean when you said, 'Please, Lord, let her body rest in Zion's graces, and let no man ever disturb this vessel, for if they do, they will meet you sooner than later'?"

"It was just a mourning father's disjointed prayer," he mumbled. "I wasn't thinking clearly."

"That fact is obvious. Men who are thinking clearly don't forget to put a body in a coffin."

The chains clanked as he lifted his manacled hand and wiped his mouth. His expression displayed a combination of fear and resignation. "What do you mean?" he finally whispered.

"You know exactly what I mean, Wilbur. I don't know why you said what you did or whether you thought anyone would understand it. But the last part of your prayer was a warning about what was really in that box. I didn't figure that out until we dug it up and opened it."

"I'm so sorry." He buried his face in his hands. When he looked up tears were streaming down his face. "I wonder if he knew that."

"If who knew what?"

"Nothing," Shellmeyer whispered, shaking his head.

Meeker looked into the man's eyes. "The charade has gone on too long, Wilbur. Two innocent men have died. You'll soon be the third."

"I'm sorry," he repeated.

"Where is Zion?"

His eyes wandered around the room. "That's where Ellen is.

She's safe in Zion. Zion is heaven."

Meeker studied him for a moment, considering his words. Suddenly she understood. Given his profession, it made perfect sense. "You're playing the role of Christ, aren't you? You're saving an innocent soul by allowing yourself to be executed."

"No," he replied, but his tone sounded more like a lie than a man committed to telling the truth.

"Okay." She leaned forward, playing a hunch that was the ultimate long shot. "What does the name Nigel Andrews mean to you?"

His frightened expression proved she had stumbled onto the truth—or at least part of it.

"Tell me what it is, Wilbur."

"He called yesterday. I got the message from the warden. But I didn't talk to him."

"Why not?"

He shook his head and remained mute.

"You aren't going to tell me any more, are you?"

He sighed. "I can't."

Meeker dropped the notebook back into her bag, picked up her purse, and moved to the door. Before reaching for the knob, she turned back. "Only Jesus can be Jesus, Wilbur. And as I remember the story, he didn't die for a lie; he died for the truth." She pointed her finger at Shellmeyer. "I know you're walking to your death because of a promise that someone made to you. But think about this, Wilbur. They can't let Ellen go. She knows who they are. If they haven't already killed her, they will the second they know you've died and can't reveal their secret."

He cringed. Clearly she'd struck a chord.

"On top of that, you're betraying your country. That's a steep price to pay for living a lie." She allowed her words to soak in. "If you give your life for this cause, it will serve absolutely no purpose. And if you take to the grave whatever it is you know, I'm betting a lot more people will die."

Sorrow filled his eyes. But no words came out of his mouth.

Meeker opened the door and walked out. Warden Dennis greeted her in the hall. "What did he tell you?"

"Not much with his words, but a great deal with his eyes." As the two walked back down the hall, she added, "I'm hoping he'll ask you to call me. You have my number."

"I do."

She stopped just outside his door. "He said you took a call from a man named Nigel Andrews."

"Yesterday, yes."

"What did he sound like?"

"A Brit."

What was the tie between Andrews and Shellmeyer? She had to find out. And that meant tracking down the English corporal before he left for England.

CHAPTER 22

A cold wind kicked up as if to remind Washington that winter was not yet over. Helen Meeker, her body exhausted but her mind still whirling, opened her apartment door at half past eight. She had no more than pulled off her shoes than the phone rang. She picked it up and was greeted by her partner's familiar baritone.

"Did you have any success with Shellmeyer?" Reese asked.

"He's still willing to die to make sure his daughter lives. And he told me very little that we don't already know."

"Well, I think I have something."

"Don't keep me waiting."

"Corporal Nigel Andrews is missing. He was scheduled to go back to England today, and he wasn't in his room at the embassy when they came to pick him up."

"So the information Reggie gave us was spot-on."

"Could be, though no one at MI6 or SIS is talking. When I called my contacts there, they refused to comment on whether

Andrews is suspected of passing information along to the Nazis. The warrant that's been issued on him is AWOL. Right now it seems to be a military matter."

Meeker glanced across the room to her front door, making sure she had remembered to lock it. "Andrews called the prison yesterday and asked to talk to Shellmeyer. Shellmeyer didn't speak with him."

"Maybe he was trying to make sure the preacher held his tongue."

"That's one possibility. Have you had any success in digging up suspicious activity in any of the Zions in the country?"

"I have two more reports I'm waiting on, but they're long shots. Looks like we're going to draw a blank there."

"Not what I wanted to hear." Meeker sighed. "We have to find that girl in order to convince Shellmeyer to give us what he's hiding."

"It might be easier to find the proverbial needle in a haystack."

"Well, needles are usually found there by sitting on them." She took a deep breath. "What about the preacher's notes and the Bible? Did you get anything out of those?"

"I deserve a bit more praise on that one," Reese bragged. "The man he was supposed to see in Mississippi is likely Russell Strickland. They roomed together in college. Strickland became a lawyer and worked awhile in the attorney general's office. About a decade ago he moved to Gulfport and set up practice there."

"So we can run him down?"

"It's not that easy. Strickland is in England now, working

with the OSS. He was too old for active service, so the US is using his skills with our intelligence department. I've sent cables to our people in London, and they're trying to locate him. As soon as I find him, I'll set up a phone call."

"We don't have much time," she reminded him.

"Believe me, I know." Fatigue clouded his voice. "One more thing. I assigned one of our agents, Collins, to go through the records of every church where Shellmeyer has pastored. I gave him the background on the case, and he'll call you if he finds anything."

"Good. Now, why don't you go home and get some sleep? We have a lot of digging to do before March sixteenth."

"Think I'll take you up on that. Good night. Sleep tight."

"You too."

Meeker set the receiver into the cradle and eased down on the edge of her bed. She had slipped off her right shoe and was rubbing her foot when she heard a knock at the door. Putting the black pump back on, she walked across the small living area to her front door. Grabbing the knob in one hand and the lock in the other, she paused. "Who is it?"

A cheery voice on the other side of the entry announced, "It's your future husband."

She smiled and shook her head at the sound of Reggie's voice. When she opened the door, she found herself gazing into the eyes of the charming Scotsman. In his right hand were a dozen red roses, and in the other a box of chocolates.

"What do you have on your mind?" she asked coyly.

"I probably shouldn't say. I don't want to get slapped before dinner."

"Dinner?"

"You owe me a dance or two, remember?"

"You have no idea how tired I am," she protested.

"Have you had supper?"

"No."

"Then that's your problem." Fister grinned. "Grab your coat. I'll buy you a steak. And after it has time to settle, we'll kick up our heels."

"You're crazy." She laughed.

"Crazy over you." The hero soldier smiled. "So, will you accept my invitation?"

"How could I refuse?"

CHAPTER 23

It was well past two when Fister returned Helen Meeker to her apartment. They lingered at the front door for a few minutes, trading small talk about the evening until he leaned over, swept her up in his arms, and kissed her … deep and long.

Pulling back at last, he whispered, "No reason for the fun to end here. After all, we don't know where we'll be next week."

Nigel Andrews might have lied about a lot of things, but he was spot-on when it came to Reggie. He was the most dynamic, irresistible man she'd ever met. Whenever she was around him, she became clay waiting for the potter.

She studied his eyes. It would be so easy to give in. Every chord in her body begged her to do so, and she might have except for one reason—Alison. Her sister looked up to her as a role model. If she gave in to temptation this easily, what kind of signal would that send to the kid?

"Not tonight, Reggie," she whispered.

"You don't mean that." He drew her close and kissed her

again. Holding her in his arms, he pulled her face into his chest. She could hear his heartbeat.

He was right. She didn't mean it. She wanted what he was offering. Either of them might die serving their country over the next few months. Didn't that trump the old moral code? Besides, Alison was in Arkansas. She would never know.

After pushing out of his arms, Meeker opened her purse with nervous fingers and pulled out her key. Feeling like a high school girl at her first prom, she stuck it into the lock. The door clicked open.

She looked into her semi-dark apartment and considered how different this night had been than any other she'd known. The scrumptious dinner, the stimulating conversation, the dancing, the walk in the park. And that kiss! Reggie Fister was a hero, and he claimed to love her. Didn't he deserve this moment?

She felt his hands on her shoulders, nudging her forward. Yes, she was ready. It was time. He was the right one, and this was the right night.

The phone rang. She flipped on the light. Suddenly the situation looked different. As he tried to move her forward, she turned, put her hand on his chest, and said, "I need to get that call. I'm sure it's important."

"But—"

She cut him off. "I had a great time. Maybe too good a time. But this is getting in the way of something important … something I have to do."

The phone rang again.

"Nothing could be more important than you and me," he

140

argued. "I'm convinced the war started just to bring us together."

The phone rang a third time.

"Good night, Reggie," she whispered, pushing him back.

As soon as he cleared the entry, she closed and latched the door. Taking a deep breath, she raced to the bedroom and caught the phone on the sixth ring.

"Helen Meeker."

"Agent Collins here. I know it's late, but Reese told me to call you if I found anything, no matter what time it was."

"I don't know whether to thank you or hate you." She sighed as she sat down on her bed.

"Excuse me?"

"Never mind. What do you have?"

"A couple of interesting things. Before Shellmeyer pastored in Newport, he was in a small New York community called Germantown. He served that church for five years. I got hold of the church records, and it took me a long time to read them. The current pastor explained that Shellmeyer had a habit of recording everything. I can even tell you what they served at each of the Fourth of July picnics."

"That fits everything I know about him. So what did you uncover?"

"About five years ago, a young man from England came over for a summer to assist the preacher."

"Was his name Nigel Andrews?"

"You beat me to it," Collins said with obvious awe.

So Shellmeyer did know Andrews.

"I've got something else. A year before Andrews came

calling, Shellmeyer had another visitor from the UK. This one was a foreign exchange student, and he spent his senior year attending the local high school. He even stayed at the pastor's home."

"What's his tie-in to this case?"

"Perhaps nothing. But it's a really strange coincidence that this student later served with Andrews on that mission in France. His name is Reggie Fister."

"You're kidding!"

"No, ma'am. And after all that's been in the media, I was surprised to find out something I didn't already know about the British hero."

"What's that?"

"He was an orphan."

Meeker's finger went to the lips Fister had so recently kissed. She let it linger there for a moment. There was so much about the man she didn't know, so much she needed to learn. "Anything else?"

"Not from church records. But there's another area I want to dig into. If I find anything I'll get back with you right away."

"Thanks," she said and placed the receiver back into its cradle.

CHAPTER 24

Thursday, March 12, 1942
The White House

After spending all day running down false leads on anyone matching the description of Ellen Shellmeyer, Helen Meeker glanced at the clock on the office wall. It was just past six in the evening.

"You still here, Miss Meeker?"

She looked up at Joan White, one of the secretaries who worked the switchboard. The short, pleasant woman in her fifties had a sweet smile that matched her kind brown eyes.

"I'm about to give up for the day. How about you?"

"On my way home now. But I wanted to give you these messages." She handed Meeker several small slips of paper. "You've missed a few calls, all but one of them from Reggie Fister. He's been phoning every hour on the hour. Not sure why Ellie didn't put the calls through to you."

"I asked her not to. I needed to try to find some kind of lead on a case I'm working on."

"No luck?"

"No. Maybe tomorrow."

Joan smiled. "The other message is from the president. He'd like you to drop by his office before you leave."

Meeker nodded. "I'll do that right now."

She checked her hair and makeup in a mirror before walking from the office wing to the main part of the presidential residence. Even though she was passing some of the most treasured elements of history, things that had awed her in the past, she barely noticed them. Her mind was too busy playing a tug-of-war between her feelings for the British hero and her inability to make even a dent in the case she had claimed as her own. She was so caught up in her thoughts she almost didn't realize when she had arrived at her destination.

She was surprised to find the door to the Oval Office open. But rather than charge in, she gently tapped on the door. As she did, Roosevelt looked up from behind his desk. His smile couldn't hide the weariness in his eyes.

"You wanted to see me?" Meeker asked.

"Come sit down." After she had taken a seat in front of the desk, he leaned back in his chair. "You haven't filled me in on either of your two projects."

She offered a weak smile. "I have nothing new on Shellmeyer. I'm still certain he's not guilty, but I can't prove it. What I've gathered on the case is interesting, but not worth wasting your time with at this moment."

"I hope we don't execute an innocent man."

"I still have a few days. Maybe something will pop up."

He raised an eyebrow. "And your assignment with the Brit?"

Meeker blushed. "It involves two British soldiers now. The first one, Andrews, is AWOL and might be a spy. But the man who returned from the dead has been entertaining."

The president grinned. "The British ambassador tells me Colonel Fister has taken quite a shine to you."

"There's little doubt about that."

"What are your feelings?"

"I'm not sure. I like him a lot, but I'm not ready to toss my heart into a relationship that seems to have no way to play out in the long run." She shook her head. "My dad used to say that love is a marathon, not a sprint. But it's hard to embrace that wisdom during times like these, when every moment seems so precious and life is so fragile."

"I understand," he said in an almost fatherly tone. "By the way, Winston is coming in this weekend. Only those directly involved are aware of it."

She nodded. "Is the meeting still planned for the Grove Estate outside of Ithaca?"

"Yes," he said, accentuating his answer with a wave of his hand. "The owners are longtime friends of my family, the farm is private and secure, and the house can easily accommodate all those who'll be there. And to keep from drawing attention to the meetings, the security details will be minimal. Your name is on the pass list if you get a chance to come."

"I'll likely be working on the Shellmeyer case."

"I thought as much. But before you leave, I'd like you to give me a bit of information on what I can expect from Colonel

Fister. He'll be at Churchill's side, and I'll likely get a chance to visit with him over dinner and during breaks."

Meeker shrugged, her eyes moving to a window as she took a deep breath. "He's rugged, charming, and very Scottish. Kind of a rogue too. He lacks some of the English reserve and is a bit more impulsive and outspoken than most Brits. He's very sure of himself and will not be intimidated by your presence."

The president nodded. "Sounds like Hollywood's version of a hero."

"Pretty close. But with a better accent."

Roosevelt chuckled. "Helen, I hope you can make it up to see us. I'd love for you to meet Churchill. He's a unique character."

"I'll do my best. If I haven't come up with anything to convince Shellmeyer to take back his confession by Monday, there'll be no reason to sit around and watch the clock tick down his final minutes."

"I hope it doesn't come to that."

A ringing phone signaled it was time for Meeker to take her leave. She moved toward the door as the president picked up the receiver.

A half hour later, she parked her Packard in the space in front of her apartment and strolled up the walk to her door. There on the steps lay several dozen roses. As she bent down to take in the fragrance of the beautiful red flowers, she noticed a note tacked to her door. The message was short and direct: "Must see you tomorrow. R. F."

CHAPTER 25
Friday, March 13, 1942

Much as she had the previous day, Helen Meeker avoided Reggie Fister's calls while she worked. Not so much because she didn't want to see him, but working with Reese on trying to track down Ellen Shellmeyer required her undivided attention. Unfortunately, the more they dug, the more she came to believe there were no needles in this haystack.

At six, after they had called it quits and were walking across the parking lot to their cars, Reese offered a piece of wisdom. "Sometimes innocent people die, and we can't do anything about it, no matter how hard we try. We may not be able to get the information we need to save Shellmeyer. But he's resigned to his fate. Maybe we should be too."

She stopped beside her Packard and shook her head. "He does not want to die. He just feels he has no choice."

"Whatever the reason, he is determined to do it."

Tears pricked her eyelids, and she blinked them back. "Do you think Ellen is still alive?"

He shook his head.

"I do. I can feel it. She's out there somewhere. I'm just afraid we're going to find her too late, and her father will have died for nothing."

"We all die for something," Reese noted. "Look, I feel for the man and his family. But Shellmeyer's death doesn't mean nearly as much to me as something else."

"What's that?"

His eyes, serious and focused, locked on hers. "I can't help but wonder how many people will die because of the information Shellmeyer is taking to his grave."

"I say, what's this all about?" Somehow Reggie Fister had snuck up on them.

"Nothing," Reese muttered, his expression clouding over. Turning on his heels he brushed by the Scotsman and marched down the walk toward his car.

"What's wrong with him?" Fister asked.

Meeker shook her head, but she knew the answer. Reese was jealous of the chemistry he saw between her and Reggie.

"Would you like to go out?" the Brit asked. "This is my last night in town. For once I'd like to make Friday the thirteenth seem lucky."

She nodded her agreement. But her eyes were still on Reese.

CHAPTER 26

After sharing dinner at a swank hotel restaurant, Helen Meeker and Reggie Fister listened to the Glenn Miller orchestra at a club downtown. When they were ready to call the public facet of the evening done, they hopped into her yellow Packard.

"I'll drop you off at the hotel," she said as she swung out of the club's parking lot.

"Why don't we head to your place instead? I can catch a cab back to the hotel later."

Against her better judgment, she pointed the car in the direction of her home. Ten minutes later she unlocked the door and they stepped inside.

"Nice place," he said as he glanced at her modest living room. "Not large, but very tasteful. The sofa looks comfortable."

He opened the door to the bedroom, flipped the switch, and glanced at the bed. Turning, he smiled and tilted his head slightly. "I like this place. I can picture you everywhere I look. Wish I'd been here before now."

"I'll bet you do," she quipped.

His cocky expression revealed that he felt sure how this night was going to end. And until a few hours ago, she might have granted his wish. But as they ate, listened to the band, and danced at the club, Fister was not the only thing on her mind. The colonel now had to share space with a certain FBI agent. Deep in her heart the two men were playing tug-of-war for her affections. The battle left her both confused and unsettled.

"Do we start out here?" Fister asked, pointing to her couch. "Or should we skip that step and move in there?" He shifted his hand in the direction of the bedroom.

"You're pretty sure of yourself." Meeker folded her arms across her chest.

He shrugged. "This could be our last night together. Who knows if we will ever meet again? We only have this moment, and we will regret it for as long as we live if we don't take advantage of it."

"Who will regret it more, I wonder."

He shook his head. "There is no one in this world like you, and I think I am pretty special too. I believe we would both miss something remarkable by not spending the rest of the night together."

Meeker knew what he meant. But the temptation she'd felt the last time was gone now. Why? What was missing? Was it her sudden realization that Reese was jealous? Or was it the fact that Shellmeyer was counting down the hours toward his meaningless death?

"Why the hesitation?" Fister closed the distance between them and slipped his arms around her.

"There's a lot going on right now," she said as she leaned away from his approaching lips.

"Forget Shellmeyer for a few hours," he whispered as he drew even closer.

His lips brushed hers, and for a moment she went limp in his arms. But she couldn't forget Wilbur Shellmeyer. He needed to be saved. He had to tell her what he knew, and she was determined to reunite that family. That was far more important than a few hours of passion. Until this case was resolved, she would not allow love, lust, or whatever this was to steal her focus.

Meeker pushed her hands into Fister's chest and freed herself from his grip. She spun on her heels, her swift action causing her hair to fly over her shoulders, and walked to the front door. She yanked it open, allowing the cool night air into the room. "You need to go."

His face registered shock. "Did I do something wrong?"

She smiled. "Without meaning to, you woke me up to what I need to be doing right now. This is not about you or me; it's about saving an innocent man's life. That's what I do. I couldn't live with myself if I didn't keep trying until the bitter end. And one night with you, no matter how tempting, is just not in the cards."

"Come on, lassie," he begged. "I might never have another kiss or get another chance to love someone. This is war, remember?"

"If all you need are lips and a body, there are a lot of women out there who would be more than happy to give in to the charms of a hero. Find the one that appeals to you the most. She'll likely take you wherever you want to go."

Fister set his jaw. "I fear you will always regret this."

"Perhaps," she admitted. "You're handsome, charming, and you earned the title of hero. But you're just a man. And while what you've done is impressive, it doesn't overrule the one thing that I just realized."

"What's that?"

"For you I'm just a conquest." She smiled. "You actually believe that you have more value than I do. You proved that when you asked me to forget my job and put you first."

His blank expression told her he had no idea what she was saying.

Meeker shook her head. "Because I'm a woman, you might see me as second rate. But in my mind I'm your equal. And if you ever want to realize your dreams about me, you'll have to treat me as if I'm every bit as important as you seem to believe you are."

"And if I don't, we'll never see each other again?"

"Maybe. Maybe not. But one thing I can guarantee is that you won't see any more of me tonight." She nodded toward the exit. "Thank you for a lovely evening."

Fister moved toward the door. He didn't bother looking back as it closed behind him.

CHAPTER 27
Saturday, March 14, 1942

Because the decision she'd made to push Fister out of her apartment and probably out of her life had been such a difficult one, Helen Meeker had a tough time getting to sleep. Just as she finally managed to drop off, the phone rang. Pulling herself back to reality, she grabbed the receiver.

"I hope this isn't a wrong number."

"It's not," her partner assured her. "I've got a lead on what might be a sighting of Ellen Shellmeyer."

Suddenly wide awake, Meeker bolted upright. "Where?"

"Zion, Pennsylvania. I've got a plane that can get us there, but we need to leave in the next hour. I'll pick you up. Can you be ready in thirty minutes?"

"Already halfway there," she assured him, leaping out of bed. "Can you bring some donuts?"

"You bet."

CHAPTER 28

Zion was a small community in the middle of the state Ben Franklin had once called home. The town was typical of rural Pennsylvania—clean, quaint, and quiet. Everyone's dream of what life in America should be.

Helen Meeker drove the car that had been waiting for her and Reese at the airport. The five-year-old Studebaker's strong motor and good tires offset its suspect styling. At just past three, the two partners pulled up to a road leading to a farmhouse about two miles outside of Zion.

"See the name on the mailbox?" Reese pointed.

James W. Grace. Meeker recalled the part of Shellmeyer's prayer when he said, "Let her body rest in Zion's graces." Could that have been code for this place? "What do we know about the folks who live here?"

"Not much. They moved to Zion last year. They've kept a low profile. About a month after they arrived, the mailman spotted a blonde teenage girl on the porch, and he caught glimpses of her through the windows from time to time. He said she never goes to town with either of the adults who live here."

Meeker turned her attention to the house at the end of the half-mile-long dirt lane. The small white frame, surrounded by trees, had a front porch about ten feet wide. The lack of adequate cover meant there was no way to approach the structure without being seen.

"So, what's your plan?"

Reese smiled. "You're canvassing for the local Lutheran church. You'll drive up to the house, knock on the door, and see if they'll let you in to answer some questions."

"And you?"

"I'll be hiding in the backseat. After you get their attention, I'll roll out of the car and check out what's inside the home through the windows. If I see the girl and she looks like Ellen, I'll catch them off guard and we'll grab her." He eased out of the passenger seat, stepped outside, and opened the back door.

"You really think it'll be that easy?"

He slid into the backseat and dropped down to the floorboard. "I guarantee it'll be far easier than seducing a British soldier."

"Hey," she grumbled as she put the car into first gear and pressed the gas pedal. "You're taking an awful lot for granted."

"I hope I'm wrong," he snapped back.

Meeker almost assured him that he was, but stopped short. For the time being it might be better to let him think the worst.

As she drove up the long lane, she scoped out the home and yard. A large yellow cat lounged on the porch rail, but thankfully, no dog appeared as she pulled into the yard. Though all of the home's shades were pulled tight, she noted a side window where someone seemed to be peeking through the gap. A bright red, mid-thirties Nash sedan was parked on the left side of the house. She pulled up beside it, figuring that would give Reese the cover he needed to escape unnoticed from their car.

After flipping off the ignition, Meeker grabbed her purse and opened the door. "Shades are drawn, so it should be easy for you to work your way up there without being spotted. But I'm not sure you'll be able to see much inside."

Reese didn't answer.

Walking around the Nash and over the thick brown grass, Meeker marched up the four steps, paused on the porch, and rapped on the door. A few moments later it opened. Filling the entry was a man, perhaps forty, about five-foot-ten and two hundred pounds. He wore slacks, dark shoes, and a white shirt. His unshaven face remained stoic as he waited for her to speak.

"Good day. My name is Helen. I'm doing a canvas for the area Lutheran churches and would like to ask you and your family a few questions about your church attendance." She looked into the man's dark eyes and studied his expressionless face.

"We don't go to church," he said.

"Perhaps that's because your church isn't giving you what you need. In these days of world war, faith is more important than ever. Don't you agree?"

He shrugged.

"Is your wife at home?"

"Step aside, Bob." A heavyset woman with a tiny chin and deep blue eyes pushed past the man. "We used to go to church, but quit a few years back."

"Well, could I come in and tell you about ours?"

The woman stepped to the side and waved her in. Meeker took a seat on a worn, wine-colored couch. To her left sat a potbellied stove; on her right, an oversized green chair, which the man sank into. The coffee table in front of her held several issues of *National Geographic*.

Meeker recalled the name on the mailbox outside the house: James W. Grace. But his wife had just called him Bob. Strange.

Glancing through the door into the kitchen, Meeker noticed a blonde girl, perhaps seventeen or eighteen, sitting at the table, folding towels. Bingo!

"Perhaps your daughter would like our youth group," Meeker suggested.

"She's shy," the woman explained. "And a bit touched in the head. She doesn't get out much."

"I see." Meeker turned her gaze back to the woman. "Tell me, why did you quit going to church?"

"We moved," came the woman's straightforward reply.

Meeker looked back at the man, who was staring out the window. She noted a bulge in his left pocket. As he pulled the sleeves of his shirt off his wrists, she saw a tattoo that looked like a ship's anchor. Had they struck pay dirt?

Through the kitchen, Meeker saw the back door open and Reese creep inside. "Mr. and Mrs. Grace, could I get your phone number? I'm sure I have a pen and paper in my purse."

As she reached into her bag, she placed her fingers around her Colt. When Reese reached the doorway, she yanked it out and aimed it at the man of the house. "Don't go for your gun."

"What are you doing?" the woman shrieked.

Meeker pointed to the kitchen. "My partner and I are here on behalf of the FBI. We have some questions about that blonde girl."

The couple glanced at Reese. "I figured you'd catch up with us at some point," the man said. "We did take the girl. But we had good reason."

"And what reason was that?"

"My brother abused her," the woman explained. "He beat her up so often and so hard that her head's not right. And her back is full of scars. The poor thing doesn't trust anybody, and she's scared of her own shadow. If we hadn't taken her and run, I truly believe she'd be dead now."

"What's her name?" Reese demanded, glancing back at the teenager, who sat at the table, continuing to fold towels.

"Suzy Mertens," the woman replied.

"Is that true?" Reese asked the girl.

She looked up and nodded, then went back to her task.

"That's what she does for hours and hours," Mrs. Grace explained. "Folds and unfolds, all day long." She shook her head. "Maybe you folks can find someone who can help her. I've tried, and I just can't."

Meeker glanced from the teen to the woman. "You called your husband Bob, but the name on the mailbox is James."

"We made up new names when we moved here from Carolina," the man said.

"What did you do in Carolina?" Reese asked.

"We were both school teachers."

Mrs. Grace reached for a scrapbook on an end table. Opening it to a particular page, she handed it to Meeker. Taped to facing pages were two teaching certificates.

Meeker turned to Mr. Grace. "What do you have in your pocket?"

He glanced down and retrieved a tobacco tin. "I roll my own."

Meeker slipped the gun back into her purse.

"I'll have to check out your story," Reese said as he put his gun away. "But for the time being, if you promise not to move from this location, we can leave the girl with you. Once we confirm she's been abused in the past, I'll find a place where she can be treated and get some help."

"Can you really do that?"

"We'll try," Meeker said. She stood and moved toward the door.

"Thank you," the woman called as her two visitors walked to the car.

Just over forty-eight hours remained before Shellmeyer would be put to death, and they had wasted an entire day on something that had no bearing on the case. On top of that, they had charged into a home where two people were doing nothing more than trying to save a child from pain and anguish. Meeker wondered if they'd ever get a break.

CHAPTER 29

Sunday, March 15, 1942
Washington, DC

Time was running out, and Helen Meeker didn't feel like she had even a prayer of saving Wilbur Shellmeyer. Then again, she hadn't actually been praying.

She felt so overcome with a sense of impotence that she couldn't sleep. After getting up and eating half a piece of toast, she called Henry Reese and asked if there were any more leads.

"We're out of Zions. I don't know what we can do that we haven't already tried."

"We're missing something," she said, her tone anything but convincing.

"But what is it, and how do we find it?"

"I don't know. But I've decided to attend the Methodist church down the street this morning. I need to put things in perspective, and I can't do it on my own. Doubt if I can in church either, but it's about the only thing I haven't tried. Could you pick up me up there around noon? I'm just going to walk and leave my car here."

"Sure. I'll see you in a couple of hours."

After dressing in a dark suit and light blue blouse, she made the five-block stroll to the gray stone building. As had been the case since war was declared, the sanctuary was almost filled. She found a spot on the edge of the pew next to the entrance and took a seat. After four hymns and two prayers, the sermon began and Meeker turned her thoughts back to Wilbur Shellmeyer.

While she had tried her best, she had done little for the man and his wife. By tomorrow evening that would be starkly clear. She wondered if his death would haunt her for the rest of her life. Over the next half hour she wondered about a lot of other things, but her jumbled thoughts only plunged her into a deep pool filled with self-pity.

She was so busy beating herself up and rehashing all she knew about the case that she wasn't even aware the service had ended until the man seated next to her stepped in front of her to leave. Even that didn't prompt her to get up. She continued to sit there until everyone had left the sanctuary.

"Are you all right?"

She looked up into the kind eyes of a man in his declining years. He was slightly built, dressed in a black suit, and balding.

"My name is George Miles. I pastored this church until I retired a few years ago. Still go here, even though I'm a civilian now. You look a bit troubled. Do you need prayer?"

"No." She sighed. "More like a miracle."

"They still happen sometimes."

"What can you tell me about Zion?" she asked.

His face took on a confused expression. "We sing about Zion in hymns. It's mentioned in the Bible, and there are sermons preached on the subject. What exactly are you looking for?"

Meeker locked her eyes on his. "What does the word mean to you, as a preacher?"

He smiled. "For most Christians today, Zion means heaven. But the early believers likely used it to refer to the Holy City. I'm more of a scholar, so when I think of Zion, I go back to ancient Jewish history, where it conjures up images of the City of David. Does that help?"

"It probably should," she muttered as she rose from the pew. "But I have no idea how to put this puzzle together."

"It'll come to you in time."

"Sadly, time is the one thing I don't have." Lowering her eyes, Meeker walked out of the church.

CHAPTER 30

Reese's FBI-issued Ford was idling at the curb when Helen Meeker exited the church and walked down its ten stone steps. He leaned across the coupe's front seat and pushed the passenger door open as she approached. "How was the service?"

"I have no idea," she admitted as she picked up the Sunday newspaper sitting on the passenger seat and took its place. "My mind was on the case. I'm still trying to figure out the code at the grave."

"Maybe it wasn't code," Reese suggested. "Maybe Shellmeyer was just spouting a few random words before he gave the grave diggers and the funeral director that cryptic warning not to open the coffin."

"You may be right."

"I heard something interesting this morning. Andrews is still missing, and the Brits have asked the FBI to help find him. We've issued an All Points for him from coast to coast. The Canadian Royal Mounted Police are even involved."

"He can't hide forever." Meeker smiled as she noticed the headlines on the newspaper in her lap. The lead stories were about Churchill meeting with his team in London and FDR getting away from town for a holiday in Warm Springs, Georgia. The charade was working beautifully.

"There's a file on Fister in the backseat," Reese said. "When I stopped at the office I ran into Collins, and he'd just finished writing it up. I told him I'd give it to you."

She reached over the seat, retrieved the folder, and pulled out the three pages of typewritten material. "Did you look through this?"

"I wanted to. But Fister is none of my business. Neither is what you do, or have done, with him."

Meeker smiled. "Well, let's just say that if it were a race, you'd be winning."

His eyes sparkled, and a smile stretched across the entire width of his face. "You mean that?"

She nodded. "He wanted more than I could give him."

"Did you want to?"

"I did … for an instant."

"What stopped you?"

"I think it was the fact that giving in to him meant not giving my all to the case. Shellmeyer is probably going to die, and there's nothing we can do about it. But if I gave up trying to save him just to indulge in something that could be saved for another place and time, what does that say about me?"

"It speaks volumes that you didn't give in to the crafty and charismatic Scotsman."

"I doubt it. But I'm glad you think so. Now, how about you take me out to eat? Maybe to a diner with some kind of greasy food."

"I know just the place." He laughed.

As Reese drove away from the curb, Meeker glanced at the file. Fister might have been an orphan, but he had a pretty good youth. After spending a year in the United States, he used the exchange program to study in Austria. After that he returned to London and joined the service. By the time the war broke out, he was an officer and seemed destined to become just what he was now—the embodiment of the ultimate English hero.

CHAPTER 31

After lunch Meeker and Reese went over every detail of the case. They spent hours trying to find something they'd missed, but came up completely dry.

Defeated and depressed, Meeker had her partner take her home, where she fixed a light supper and turned on the radio. The war news did nothing to improve her mood. A German U-boat had sunk a British naval ship in the North Sea, killing more than a hundred sailors. Another Nazi sub sank a US tanker a few miles off the North Carolina coast. MacArthur had been flown out of the Philippines. The general's leaving seemed the ultimate act of surrender.

She shut off her radio, picked up her phone, and asked for the long-distance operator. After being shifted from one operator to another, she finally heard the phone ring at her sister's dormitory. It took the dorm mother two minutes to find Alison.

"Hey, Sis," she almost shouted.

"How are you doing, kid?"

"Great! I love it here at Ouachita. Best semester ever!"

"Does that mean you've found a boyfriend?"

Alison laughed. "You told me not to settle down yet. But yeah, I've had a few dates."

"Good. I want you to have fun. How are your grades?"

"No problems there at all. How are you doing?"

Meeker leaned back in her bed and sighed. "I'm struggling with a difficult case. I just can't get a good grasp on it. I feel like the answer is right in front of me, but I can't see it."

"I'm sure you'll figure it out. You always do."

"Maybe not this time."

"Hey, you found me, remember? Everyone believed I was dead, but not you. You knew I was alive."

"I just *felt* like you were."

"And how do you feel now?"

Meeker paused, considering the question. "I feel like the person I'm looking for is alive."

Alison laughed. "That's the spirit! You know, one of my professors says that life is a pilgrimage, and we just have to keep going until we find out where we're supposed to be."

Meeker chuckled. "That's a bit too vague for a logical mind like mine. Besides, I've got less than a day to get to where I have to be. If I don't complete my pilgrimage by then, it won't matter."

"Well, maybe you're not following the right map," Alison suggested. "The world's top destinations for pilgrimages are Mecca and Jerusalem. Maybe you should try going to one of those places instead of wherever you're stuck now."

"Alison, you might just be brilliant!"

"Really?"

"I love you, but I've got to go. I think you just gave me the clue I needed."

"Glad I could help, even if I don't know what I did."

"I'll talk to you later. Good night."

"I love you, Helen."

"I love you too, kid."

As soon as the line went dead, Meeker hit the button to get a dial tone. She then called Reese. He answered after only two rings.

"Henry, I think I might know what city Ellen Shellmeyer is in."

"Super!"

"Can you leave with me tonight?"

"Sorry. I've been assigned to run down a lead on Nigel Andrews. He was just seen in Baltimore. I'm about to leave. But where do you think she is?"

Helen smiled. "Zion."

"As in heaven?"

"As in the City of David."

"Jerusalem?"

"That's right."

"You're going to the place where Jesus died?"

"A little closer. I'm headed for Jerusalem, New York."

"Sounds like a hunch."

"It's a long shot. But it's the only shot I've got."

"Well, be careful. And call in backups. Don't try to do this alone."

"Once I'm sure I've figure it out right, I'll get the locals to help me. But right now I need to pack a bag, get a bath, put on some clean clothes, and go. I'm heading off on an all-night pilgrimage."

CHAPTER 32

Monday, March 16, 1942
Jerusalem, New York

Intense blowing rain plagued Helen Meeker during her entire road trip. At times the wipers couldn't keep up, and the gale-force winds almost pushed her off the road more times than she could count. As a result, the trip took much longer than she had planned.

At just past ten in the morning, she pulled into the hamlet of Jerusalem. The sign claimed a population just over two thousand.

She drove each of the city's streets, studying the various homes and businesses. She knocked on dozens of doors and showed folks the picture of Ellen Shellmeyer. No one could help.

One hour became two, two became three, and nothing jumped out as being the place where the girl might be being held. At one in the afternoon Meeker finally pulled into a local diner to grab a bite to eat and try to regain her focus.

She had no more than sat down when a middle-aged, dark-haired waitress wearing a dress one size too small sidled up to her booth. "What do you want?" She snapped her gum while she waited.

"Could I get a ham sandwich?"

"Sure. On white?"

"That'd be fine."

"You want it fully loaded? Lettuce, tomato, onion?"

Meeker shook her head. "No, thanks. Just mayo. And a Coke."

"I'll have them out in about five minutes."

As the woman started to turn, Meeker stopped her. "Do you have a phone book I can look at?"

"Sure. I'll grab it and bring it right back to you."

In less than sixty seconds the waitress returned to the table with the small book. Mentally reciting the pastor's unusual graveside prayer, *Please, Lord, let her body rest in Zion's graces,* Meeker flipped to the Yellow Pages. Sadly, there were no local businesses with "rest" in their name. So she went to the white pages and looked up individuals' names. She was up to the *e*'s when the waitress delivered her order.

"Thanks." After taking a few bites of the sandwich, Meeker looked up at the clock. She had less than five hours to find the Shellmeyer girl and stop her father's execution.

If the clue to where she was couldn't be traced to the word *rest*, then where was the answer? Meeker considered each word of the pastor's prayer. She even tried mixing up the words to find the right combination. "Please body. Lord body. Lord rest."

She was still going through her word-scramble exercise when the waitress came back to the booth. The woman shook her head and smiled. "I was a kid when that place was in its prime."

"What place?"

"The old estate house," the waitress explained between chomps on her gum.

"What estate house?"

"The one you were mumbling about—The Lord's Rest. It was a horse farm, named after the greatest racehorse the original owner ever bred. But it went under back in the 1920s. It's been abandoned for years. It's kind of a spooky three-story mansion. Folks around here call it the haunted house."

"Where is it?"

"You go a mile down the road to Oak Street. Turn right there and continue till you pass a couple of vacant businesses. Make a left on a dirt road and go about a quarter of a mile. It's muddy today, so you might get stuck. Anyway, you can't see it from the road because of the trees that have grown up."

"Thanks," Meeker said, glancing out the window into the pouring rain. As she did, the diner's lights flashed off and then back on.

"That's been happening a lot today," the waitress explained. "If this storm keeps up, we'll lose power for sure."

"What do I owe you?" Meeker asked.

"Sixty-five cents."

As she rose, Meeker tossed down a five-dollar bill. "Keep the change."

"Wow," the waitress whispered. "Thanks."

As Meeker pulled on her coat, the waitress said, "Oh, there's something else you might need to know. Someone bought that old place last year. They said they were going to fix it up, but they haven't done much yet. It does have power, though. And there are some folks who stay there from time to time. I've never met any of them."

"I can't tell you how much I appreciate this." Meeker pushed by the woman and rushed out into the rain.

CHAPTER 33

Helen Meeker had just pulled out of the diner's parking lot when the lights went out all over town. As dark as the skies were and as hard as the rain was falling, it seemed more like night than early afternoon. With the Packard's wipers speeding up and slowing down depending on the motor's demands, Meeker had a difficult time seeing the road. She missed the first turn and had to make a trip around the block to correct her mistake.

A half mile later she passed the two vacant businesses and spotted where she needed to be. She pulled into the lane and parked her car under a large elm tree just to the right of a dirt trail. Reaching over the front seat, she grabbed a set of rubber boots, a raincoat, and an umbrella from the backseat. After taking her gun out of her purse and dropping it into her jacket pocket, she put on the slicker and boots, slid out of the car, and popped open the umbrella. Fighting both wind and rain, she pushed forward through the mud. Halfway down the lane, a wind gust turned her umbrella inside out. Meeker tossed it aside and moved on.

The ancient Victorian home looked like something out of the 1800s. At one time it must have been a real showplace, but now its wraparound porches were sagging, shutters were either gone or hanging sideways, and there was very little paint left on the wood siding.

Meeker couldn't just walk up on the porch, knock on the door, and ask if Ellen Shellmeyer was in the house. She needed a plan.

As she hid behind a large oak and considered her options, she recalled a promise she'd already broken. She had forgotten to call the local cops for backup. There was no time to correct that oversight now. The clock was ticking, and she had only a short window of opportunity to save a man's life.

The pouring rain was joined by massive bolts of lightning, followed by loud blasts of thunder. But Meeker saw the storm as a godsend because it made for a great cover.

Opting to circle around the house in order to peer into a few windows and get the lay of the land, Meeker moved toward the old mansion. The first three rooms were void of furniture. The next was a large living room where two men, dressed in slacks and white shirts, sat in old, well-used high-backed chairs. This room also contained a desk, a few other chairs of similar style, and an antique Victorian couch. While there were several lamps and two overhead light fixtures, the room was lit only by two candles. The men, seemingly unconcerned about the weather, were smoking cigars and drinking a dark-colored liquid. She guessed it to be whiskey or scotch.

A DATE WITH DEATH *In the President's Service Series: Episode 1*

As she studied the scene, she focused closely on the men. They both fit Virginia Shellmeyer's descriptions of the ones who'd posed as funeral directors at the graveside. Satisfied she had the right location, Meeker circled the rest of the home to see if there were any more men she had to worry about. Besides the duo, she saw no one else on the ground level. If Ellen was there, she must be on either the second or third floor.

The kitchen seemed to be the most logical point of entry. Sneaking up onto the back steps, she tried the door. It was locked. Pushing her wet hair off her face, she moved back to the muddy ground and tried four windows. They were all locked too.

A flash of lightning struck a nearby tree, and the rolling thunder that followed almost split her eardrums. That gave her an idea. Pulling her gun from her inside jacket pocket, she moved to a window as far from the men as possible. She waited beside it until a flash of lightning lit up the sky. When the thunder roared two seconds later, she shattered the window with the butt of her gun.

After brushing away the remaining glass, she grabbed the window fame and pulled herself inside. After dropping to the floor, she moved into the shadows to see if the storm's fury had managed to cover her actions. She waited thirty seconds, gun drawn, before she breathed.

The kitchen was to her left. She noted the door and considered her options. When she'd peered in from the outside, she'd spotted a stairway in a hall outside the kitchen. While it was close to the room where the men were relaxing, if she was quiet she could likely make it up the winding stairs without them detecting her presence.

After setting her gun on the table, she yanked off her boots and pushed them under a chair. Then she removed the raincoat and laid it on the wooden plank floor. Picking up her Colt, she silently crossed the room in her stocking feet.

Leaning into the door she gently pushed it open, then stepped into a large kitchen that would have been modern in 1890. The cabinets were minimal and painted white. Beyond a couple of old-fashioned food cabinets against a far wall, there was a fairly up-to-date refrigerator. A six-by-four-foot table sat in the middle of the room, with two stools pushed under it. In the center of the table was an oil lamp filled with kerosene. It was lit, and the steady flame provided some light.

Meeker snuck across the kitchen to an open door leading to the hall. She hugged the wall until she got to the steps, then glanced into the living room. Neither man was looking her way. She climbed the winding, eight-foot-wide wooden staircase. Only one of the twenty planks creaked, and with the rain pouring down, she figured that noise was likely not noticed.

The second floor had eight rooms, four on each side, separated by a ten-foot-wide hall. The four rooms on the left were empty. They didn't even have furniture. The first room at the back of the hall was the same. The next was furnished, and some men's clothing lay on a couch. The third was a bathroom, dirty but functional. The final room on this floor was evidently where the other man slept. At the end of the hall was another set of stairs. These were much narrower.

After climbing the fifteen steps, she emerged into another

dark hallway. On the left were two doors, to the right were three. The first two on the right were void of anything. The third door was locked. Silently falling to her knees, Meeker peered through the keyhole. She spotted a bed, two chairs, and a chest of drawers. Standing to the right, looking out the window, was a young woman dressed in a ragged dress. She was barefoot.

Setting her gun on the floor, Meeker reached into her wet hair and pulled out a bobby pin. It was time to put her Girl Scout training to good use, though this was a skill one of the other scouts had taught her and she hadn't earned a merit badge for it.

In less than a minute she'd picked the lock. After tossing the pin aside, she grabbed her Colt, stood, and opened the door. The girl whirled, her face drawn and her expression fearful.

Meeker slipped her gun back into her jacket pocket and pressed her finger to her lips. Walking quickly to the blonde's side, she placed her hands on the captive's shoulders and whispered, "I'm here to get you out of this place. Do you understand?"

She nodded, her blue eyes displaying a blend of trust and apprehension.

"Are you Ellen Shellmeyer?"

She nodded again.

"We have to sneak out quietly. Can you do that?"

"Yes," she whispered.

"Follow me."

With Meeker leading the way, the pair exited the room. After making sure the coast was clear, they slowly made their way down the hall toward the stairway. They had covered half the distance when a man stepped out of one of the empty rooms on the far side of the hall. He had a face only a mother could love and a smile that would have scared a goblin. He was big, sported an ugly scar beneath one eye, and had an ear that looked as though it had once been a dog's chew toy. But at this moment, the gun he held was his most impressive feature.

"Who are you?" he barked.

"I'm from the office of the president of the United States, and I'm taking this girl with me."

He sneered. "I was considering killing you before. But if what you say is true, you just signed your own death warrant, lady."

His smile vanished as he aimed his gun at her. A second later a shot rang out, and smoke filled the hall. A confused look framed the man's face as he stared at the hole in Meeker's jacket, which had come from the inside out.

Yanking the still-smoking Colt into the open, Meeker watched the man fall to his knees and then forward onto his face.

She grabbed the girl's hand. "We've got to move."

After rushing down the stairs, they emerged into the second-floor hall. The other man wasn't there. Meeker charged down the winding staircase, with Ellen on her heals. Making a U-turn, she rushed toward the kitchen. As she charged into the room, a man greeted her, gun drawn and ready for action.

"Drop it, lady, or I shoot you and then the girl."

Meeker lowered her weapon. As she dropped it to the floor, she moved a step to her right so the length of the table was between them.

"That's a good girl," the man said. "I take it you killed my friend."

"Probably," Meeker admitted. "He's lying facedown in the third-floor hall. Look, you don't want to fool with me. I'm on FDR's staff. Kill me and the entire force of the United States government will be on your tail."

He grinned. "If I don't get rid of you, that'll still be the case." He aimed the gun at her head and studied her face, as if waiting for her to beg for her life.

A massive bolt of lightning struck the house, and a blast of earth-shaking fury rattled the ancient home's windows. In that split second, Meeker grabbed the edge of the table and shoved it forward, striking her adversary just below the waist. She continued to push until he was pinned between the table and the cabinet. As he bent forward in pain, Meeker picked up the oil lamp and smashed it over the hand holding the gun. The flame jumped from the wick to the oil covering the man's arm. He screamed in pain and dropped his weapon.

Meeker shoved the shocked girl toward the door. "Get out of here. I'll be right behind you." Glancing back toward the man, she watched the flame spreading across his pants and up his shoulder.

Meeker grabbed her gun. As she did, he pushed the table away and lunged toward her. She slid her stocking-covered feet to one side. The man slipped and fell into the kerosene that had dripped onto the floor. A second later the fire reached him. He rolled around on his belly, screaming.

Meeker spun toward the door and raced out into the rain. The girl was waiting for her in the yard.

"Let's go," Meeker shouted as she pointed down the lane.

Glancing back toward the home, she noted through a window that the kitchen was a wall of flame. Even with the heavy rain, this fire would not go out until the structure had burned completely to the ground. Soon The Lord's Rest would be haunted no more.

CHAPTER 34

After dragging Ellen Shellmeyer down the lane and pushing the girl into the Packard, Helen Meeker drove to the local police station. Leaving the teenager in the car, she barged through the door a little past three a.m. A sheriff and deputy were sitting behind their desks.

"I'm Helen Meeker," she announced. She pulled her credentials out of her purse and tossed them toward the man in charge. "I've just rescued a young woman from kidnappers who were holding her in the old place known as The Lord's Rest."

The sheriff stared at her credentials in disbelief. "You work for FDR?"

"Yes, I do. There are two dead men in that old house, and it's on fire."

"Wow," the deputy exclaimed.

"I need to use your phone to call the federal prison in Lewisburg, Pennsylvania."

The sheriff handed Meeker her credentials. "I'd love to help you, but the storm has knocked out the power and phone service all over the central and western parts of the state. Even our radios aren't working."

"How long does it take to drive to Lewisburg?"

"It's almost a hundred and fifty miles. Even in good weather with a powerful car, it takes almost four hours."

"Then I'll do my best to set a new speed record."

"What's the hurry?"

"Got to save a man's life. Maybe I'll get lucky and run into a place in northern Pennsylvania where the phones are working."

Meeker ran back out into the rain, hopped into her Packard, and backed out onto the street. As the car picked up speed, she glanced at the young woman in the passenger seat. "Hang on. This is going to be a wild ride. And if you know any prayers, now's the time to say them."

CHAPTER 35

Helen Meeker pushed the Packard to the limit, sliding around curves, racing through small towns, and pushing the gas pedal to the floor on long, straight stretches. A dozen times she almost lost control in the heavy rain, and on each of those occasions her frightened passenger looked at her as if she were mad. And perhaps she was. Yet she had to do whatever she could to save an innocent man's life. If she failed to make it, at least she would know she tried.

The storm had knocked out power and phone service not only in New York, but most of Pennsylvania.

At just past six, when Meeker practically flew into Lewisburg, the rain was finally starting to let up. If the execution had been carried out on time, it was already too late to save Wilbur Shellmeyer. But more often than not, these exercises in justice were delayed. Perhaps she still had a chance.

She glanced at the confused and scared girl in her passenger seat. How she wished she had the time to sit down and explain the situation to her. Instead, after stealing her from her kidnappers and killing two men right in front of her, she had taken her on a ride that made the Indianapolis 500 look like a Sunday drive in the park. But at least she was here. Soon the kid would be reunited with her family.

Pulling up to the prison gate, Meeker ordered Ellen to stay in her seat until she called for her. Then she raced over to the nearest guard. "I need to see the warden right away. I've got evidence that will overturn the conviction of a man on death row."

"Sorry, lady. You have to be on the list to get in."

Meeker opened her purse and yanked out her credentials. The guard looked them over. "You're Helen Meeker?"

"Yes. And if you'll check your records, you'll discover I was here last Wednesday. Now, do whatever it is you have to do, but I must see Mr. Dennis immediately."

The uniformed man stepped back into his booth and picked up the phone. While he was speaking, Meeker opened the door to the small room and pushed her way in. Grabbing the receiver from the stunned guard, she pulled it to her mouth. Her words flew out like blasts from a machine gun. "Warden Dennis, this is Helen Meeker. You have to stop the execution. I have Ellen Shellmeyer. Her father will talk as soon as he sees she's safe."

"Miss Meeker," Dennis said, his voice tense. "I wish you'd gotten her here ten minutes earlier. Mr. Shellmeyer has already been executed."

Meeker's throat constricted in pain. It couldn't be true!

"I'll instruct the guard to let you in. His wife is here. I'm sure she will get some relief in seeing her daughter again."

Meeker handed the receiver back to the man and slowly exited the tiny room. As she made her way back to the Packard, she didn't feel the rain or note the cool wind. She'd failed. She'd found the answer to the puzzle, but too late.

After opening the car door, she slid into the driver's seat as the huge gates swung open. She drove to the same parking space she'd used last week. After switching off the motor, she looked over to the disheveled young woman beside her. "Your mother is waiting for you inside."

A guard escorted the pair from the car to the warden's office, where Dennis was waiting for them. So was Virginia Shellmeyer, dressed in black and looking even thinner and paler than she had last week. Her eyes red and her face drawn, the woman opened her arms. The girl raced into them.

The reunion should have been infused with happiness. But Meeker's heart was bathed in pain and anguish. The father should have been able to feel his daughter's arms and see her face. But he was dead. And all because Meeker had taken too long to decipher a code.

"Miss Meeker?"

She turned her eyes from the bittersweet reunion to the warden, who stood close beside her. "Yes?"

"I thought you might want to know what Mr. Shellmeyer's final words were. They were ... strange, to say the least."

"How so?"

"After saying good-bye to his wife and pleading for God's mercy for 'living a lie,' he called out, 'God save the president and Mr. Churchill.'"

What did that mean? Was he trying to prove his loyalty to the Allies and recant his confession? She shook her head. "It's not that strange. I mean, I've read far more bizarre final statements."

"Those were not quite the last words he said. There was a postscript directed just to you."

Her heart lurched. "What was it?"

The warden whispered, "'Tell FDR's woman to unmask the imposter before he kills them.'"

Meeker considered the message. The imposter had to be Andrews. Shellmeyer knew him. And he was currently missing, with a nationwide search going on for him. But who did Shellmeyer think Andrews was going to kill?

"Oh." The warden raised a finger. "And just before the lines went down, an FBI agent named Henry Reese left a message for you. He seemed to think you'd be here before the execution."

Well, he was almost right. "What did he say?"

"He told me to tell you, 'The bird has been sighted in Elmira and is on the move.' Does that make any sense to you?"

As a map of New York took shape in her brain, she started to panic. "I need to use your phone."

"Sorry. Service is still out all over Pennsylvania and New York. I hear it might be a day or more before anyone in this area can make any calls."

"But the guard used a phone to call you."

"That was on our in-house system."

"I need a New York map."

"There's one in my desk." The warden crossed the room,

opened a drawer, and pulled out a map. After studying it, Meeker checked the office's wall clock.

"Okay," she said, more to herself than the warden. "It's six thirty. Even at top speed, it'll take more than three hours to cover the distance. But it's the only way."

"The only way to do what?"

"No time to explain. Have the guard open the gates. I'm in a hurry!"

CHAPTER 36

Helen Meeker drove out of the prison gates and pointed the Packard north. While the rain had slowed from monsoon intensity to gentle showers, the slick pavement and the darkness made driving just as dangerous as it had been on her trip to the federal correctional facility. While she'd arrived too late to save the life of an innocent preacher, perhaps she could beat the odds now and save the lives of the Allies' most powerful leaders.

As she pushed the gas pedal to the floor, she paid no attention to either the road conditions or the speed limits. While most highway signs listed a maximum speed of forty-five, Meeker doubled that. Except for slipping off the shoulder once in northern Pennsylvania, she had no problem keeping her car on the pavement.

She was five miles north of Elmira, over three-quarters of her trip completed, when a New York state patrolman gave chase. She grudgingly pulled over. Before he'd managed to walk up to her window, she was ready with her credentials. He looked them over, checked her license, and sent her on her way with a request to exercise caution. She ignored it.

At just past ten thirty she pulled into the lane leading to the Grove Estate. In spite of the steady rain, a Secret Service man raised his arm, stepped into her path, and demanded she stop. As he walked to the driver's side of the Packard, she rolled down her window. "I'm Helen Meeker. I'm on your pass list. I have important information to give to the president."

The man shined a flashlight in Meeker's face, causing her to squint, then flashed it down to her car.

"Hello, Miss Meeker," he said with a smile. "Sorry I didn't recognize your car, but I've never seen it all covered with mud."

"Since the phone lines are down, I've been driving like crazy to get here."

"Go on in. I'll radio ahead so the front-door guard will let you in the house."

"Thanks." Meeker headed down the long, paved road. After parking in front of the house, she grabbed her purse, stepped out into the rain, and rushed to the front door. A man she knew well opened it for her.

"Where's the president?"

"He and Churchill are in the back study," John said, "and he left word not to be disturbed. It's all very hush-hush. Barnes and I are the only agents in the house. And there's only one other person in the room with them. A Brit."

Meeker started down the hall. "On the right or left?"

"The left," he shouted. "But it's locked."

Stopping in front of the entry, Meeker rapped on the walnut

door.

"Who is it?" Clay Barnes's gruff voice demanded.

"Helen Meeker. I need to see the president. It's urgent."

A moment later the latch was flipped, and a tall, stern Secret Service agent opened the door. Meeker pushed by him. The president and prime minister sat on a couch on the far side of the study. Reggie Fister leaned against the wall to the right, smirking at her.

"Helen." The president sent her a sly grin. "You look like you've been playing in the rain."

Meeker glanced into the huge mirror on the wall to her right. Her shoes and stockings were splattered with mud. Her suit was damp and wrinkled. Her face was dirty, her makeup smeared, and her hair wet and stringy. "Sorry I'm not at my best, sir."

Roosevelt chuckled. "Winston, this is the beautiful young woman I was telling you about."

Churchill lifted his eyebrows. "Your definition of beauty and mine seem a bit different."

The president and Barnes laughed. Meeker failed to see the humor.

"Sit down, Helen," her boss suggested. As she took a seat in a high-backed leather chair, Roosevelt picked up the phone. "Could you bring us some coffee, please?"

With all eyes still on her, Meeker avoided everyone's stares by looking around the study. By estate standards it was small, not more than fifteen by fifteen feet. Besides the door she'd come in, the only other one was at the back of the room. One wall was nothing but bookshelves. A print of Washington crossing the

Delaware, framed in brass, was the highlight of another wall. The chairs and couches were covered with green leather, and the room's end tables were dark walnut. The paneling appeared to be cherry. The light-green carpet was plush. The filled ashtrays and lingering smell of cigars proved the men had been taking advantage of Cuba's most famous export.

Roosevelt lifted his eyebrows high enough that they rose above his glasses. "I know I invited you to come to this meeting, but I'm guessing there's a reason behind your late-night arrival."

She nodded. "Wilbur Shellmeyer was executed tonight."

The president shook his head. "I'm sorry."

"He was a spy." Fister pushed off the wall. "People who work against their countries must pay the ultimate price, especially during times of war."

A steward, dressed in a white jacket and black pants, entered through the back door. He carried a silver tray with five coffee cups, a pitcher, creamer, bowl of sugar, and plate of cookies. Without a word he set them on a table in front of the two world leaders, then stepped away until his back was against the bookshelves.

With everyone else's eyes on the tray, only Meeker noticed the man reach under his coat and yank a pistol from his belt. She unsnapped her purse and pulled out her Colt. Fister produced a gun as well … with a silencer screwed onto the barrel.

"Andrews," the Scotsman snarled.

"Nigel?" Meeker couldn't believe she hadn't recognized him.

"You can't stop me," Andrews answered. "I can easily get

off at least one shot before anyone takes me down."

"Nigel, what are you doing?" she asked.

"This has to end. Someone has to stop the needless slaughter and all the lies."

"You don't have what it takes to end it, son," Fister replied. "Put the weapon down."

Andrews shook his head and aimed at the men in the room. Fister fired first.

The blast caught Andrews in the chest. He looked down at the blood spreading across his white coat for a moment before dropping his weapon and falling forward.

"Good job, Reggie!" Churchill exclaimed.

Barnes bent over the wounded victim. Meeker aimed her gun at the English army hero.

"You can relax, Helen," Fister said. "We nailed the traitor. Thanks for coming here to warn us he was in the area."

Meeker kept her Colt pointed at Fister's face. "Lower your weapon, Reggie."

"You first."

"What's this all about?" Roosevelt demanded.

Meeker stared Fister down. "Shellmeyer's last words were about an imposter. Somehow he figured out that the Nazis had a spy in our midst."

"It was Nigel." Fister pointed at his wounded comrade. "He hated war and was willing to sell out his country to end it. He wormed his way into a job where national security information would be at his fingertips, and he passed it along to Hitler. When he heard about this meeting, he must have figured he could cripple our war efforts by assassinating both Mr. Churchill and Mr. Roosevelt." Reggie shook his head. "I have to admit, passing himself off as my best friend to grab the spotlight and then turning it into a chance for revenge was brilliant."

"Yes," Meeker said, "it was brilliant. But Nigel isn't the only Brit Shellmeyer knew. You lived in his home as an exchange student."

Fister nodded. "Yes, he knew both of us. But he must have recognized Andrews's lack of character."

She narrowed her eyes at Reggie. "Last Tuesday at Rigatti's, how did you know I was in danger in New York the day before?"

"Your secretary told me."

"She couldn't have. She didn't know. And later that same night, you told me to forget the Shellmeyer case. But I hadn't shared anything about it with you."

"I overheard you and Reese," Fister argued, his gun still aimed at her.

Meeker shook her head. "Shellmeyer didn't leave a message about a spy. His final words were about an imposter."

"Clearly, he was referring to Andrews. Helen, why can't you accept that we got the bad guy?"

She allowed herself a grim smile. "The real Reggie Fister was an orphan who lived with the Shellmeyers for a year before going off to school in Austria. That's where you met him. You'd grown up in an orphanage too, and you looked enough like him to fool Shellmeyer into believing you were him."

"This is preposterous," Fister countered. But Meeker detected beads of sweat forming on his forehead.

"The deception worked ... until the American newspapers ran a picture of you. That was when Shellmeyer grew suspicious. When the Nazi agents you were working for discovered he had arranged to meet an old friend from the attorney general's office to discover your true identity, they put a plan in action to keep the family quiet. And it almost worked."

"What are saying, Helen?" Roosevelt asked.

She pointed at Reggie. "This man, not Andrews, is the Nazi plant."

CHAPTER 37

Helen Meeker kept Reggie in the sights of her gun, waiting for him to either flinch so she could shoot him or admit she had him dead to rights. After more than a minute of uncomfortable silence, the unmasked hero finally spoke.

"You're smarter than I thought you were, Helen."

"You're not the first person to misjudge me," she assured him. "It must have been painful to be intentionally shot three times as a cover for injuries you supposedly received that night in France."

"Not as bad as you might think," he admitted. "They put me under, and the flesh wounds didn't do any real damage."

Meeker nodded at her boss and his guest, her gun still trained on Reggie. "Was this why they planted you—to kill two world leaders?"

"Not originally." He grinned. "I was only supposed to work my way inside Churchill's inner circle and then feed information back home. This opportunity fell into our laps."

"Put the gun down, Fister," Churchill ordered.

"No way. I'm walking out of here."

Meeker raised an eyebrow. "Not likely. You're either leaving this room a captive or dead. Either way is fine by me."

Fister grinned. "We have Henry Reese, Helen. He's alive. But if you want to see him again, you'll have to let me go."

Meeker swallowed the panic that threatened to close her throat. "Your plan won't work," she replied as calmly as she could. "Henry would rather die than let you go free."

His grin broadened. "We also have your sister."

Meeker felt weak. Her hands shook. "You're bluffing."

"We yanked her out of her dorm earlier today. Room 201. Her roommate's name is Rachel. Nice girl."

Apparently he wasn't bluffing. Meeker wished the phone lines were working so she could call the school and confirm it.

"If I'm not at the pickup site before ten o'clock on Friday night, both Reese and Alison will be killed."

Meeker glanced at the president. Roosevelt nodded, then looked at Barnes. "Lower your gun." The agent did as directed.

"Smart move," Fister said. "Now it's your turn, Helen."

Duty or love? It was a question she never believed she would have to answer. Was she willing to sacrifice her sister for the good of the country? Alison was young, innocent, and the only family Meeker had left. The kid had her whole life in front of her. And they'd just found each other. How could she give her up?

But the country was at war against a foe that was killing

thousands each day. Was Alison more important than all the other innocent young people being sacrificed every minute, simply because she was the sister of someone who worked for the president?

"I'm not dropping my gun," Meeker finally said. "If I did, you'd have a clear shot at the president and the prime minister."

"I would expect no less from you, Helen." Fister made his way across the room toward the back door. "You are a worthy opponent, my dear. I am sure we will meet again."

She certainly hoped not.

At the door, he looked at the others in the room. "No one had better follow me, or those two hostages will die."

"How do we know you won't kill them anyway?" Barnes asked.

"I give you my word as a Scottish gentleman."

As his left hand found the doorknob, Meeker squeezed the trigger. Smoke and noise filled the room. The bullet penetrated Fister's right wrist. He screamed. As soon as the Scot's gun fell to the floor, Meeker kicked it away.

Holding his right wrist with his left hand, the fallen hero stared up at her. "Why did you do that?"

"You're not Scottish, and you're certainly not a gentleman. So your word means nothing."

Other agents rushed into the room as Meeker hurried to the president. "We've got less than a week to find them."

Roosevelt nodded. "Do you have a plan?"

"I need to head to Arkansas before the trail goes cold. Can you get me a special plane?"

"Of course."

"In the meantime, have our men work Fister over and see if he'll talk. He probably won't, but try it anyway."

Meeker glared at Reggie. The Secret Service agent had him in handcuffs and was wrapping a handkerchief around his wrist to stop the bleeding.

Fister leered at Helen. "You won't find her."

"Never underestimate an American woman—especially this one."

While her words were honest and filled with grit, Meeker wondered if she had the time, resources, and intelligence to find the two people she cared for most in the world before it was too late. She was sure of only one thing: if she failed, it would probably kill her.

The President's Service Series

  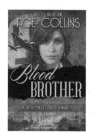

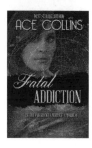 

61169636R00114

Made in the USA
Charleston, SC
17 September 2016